PU**

SWEET **

When Fran comes to live ~~~~~~~~ ~~~~~~~~ Residential Home, she can't believe her g~~~~ luck. For the first time in her life she has a room of her own which she can decorate exactly how she likes. Paralysed from the waist down and confined to a wheel-chair, she realizes she hasn't much of a future, yet she desperately wants to be treated like an ordinary teenager.

Despite her disability and the disapproval of well-meaning adults, Fran's lively nature leads her to make things happen and soon she's involved in a plan to help the bitter and withdrawn Hawkins, an eighteen-year-old boy who has lost both legs in a road accident.

The story of how Fran gets on with the other residents and how her relationship develops with Hawkins makes for a touching and at times funny novel. Independent, sometimes aggressive and moody, often mischievous, Fran is a wonderfully real character with a zest for life and a fierce courage that most readers will find both moving and inspirational.

Sweet Frannie was runner-up in the first Young Observer/ Rank Organization fiction prize.

SUSAN SALLIS

SWEET
FRANNIE

PUFFIN BOOKS

Puffin Books, Penguin Books Ltd, Harmondsworth, Middlesex, England
Penguin Books, 625 Madison Avenue, New York, New York 10022, U.S.A.
Penguin Books Australia Ltd, Ringwood, Victoria, Australia
Penguin Books Canada Ltd, 2801 John Street, Markham, Ontario, Canada L3R 1B4
Penguin Books (N.Z.) Ltd, 182–190 Wairau Road, Auckland 10, New Zealand

First published by William Heinemann Ltd 1981
Published in Puffin Books 1983

Copyright © Susan Sallis, 1981
All rights reserved

Set in Linotron Bembo by
Rowland Phototypesetting Ltd
Bury St Edmunds, Suffolk
Made and printed in Great Britain by
Cox & Wyman Ltd, Reading

CHAPTER ONE

As soon as I got to Thornton Hall I knew it was going to be different. For one thing it was a proper home, built by Sir Richard Thornton for his enormous family. It had gardens and its own chapel and a reedy lake, besides a 1972 swimming pool and modern block with all mod-cons.

I arrived one early evening in June, met the boss-man, Doctor Douglas Beamish, and politely refused his offer of formal introductions all round. He looked warmly serious and used his favourite word. 'You'd prefer to integrate slowly?' And I came back, 'Infiltrate, I think. Yes, I'll infiltrate.' He liked that and almost smiled.

Anyway the very next day I inherited a married couple from a girl who was at Thornton Hall before me and died. This couple – the Parrishes – couldn't have any children apparently, so they joined the Friends of Thornton Hall and took an interest in one boy and one girl. Straight-away they wanted me to call them Aunt Nell and Uncle Roger. I'd never had a pair of Friends of my own before, so I didn't think it would be too difficult, especially when I could stop them treating me as if I was six and slightly mental.

'Now Frances, dear –' Did her soft, breaking voice ever call me anything but Frances, dear? 'We can never be *parents* to you of course. But we'd like to be more than ordinary aunt and uncle. We'd like to be friends. You'll have lots, of course. But we'd like to be *special*. People you can talk to – confide in –'

'Friends,' I confirmed, nodding encouragingly.

She looked pleased and surprised. 'Yes. Friends.'

I met Uncle Roger's wishy-washy grey eyes and wondered if there was a laugh somewhere down there. There certainly wasn't in Aunt Nell's wide-open blue ones. She was so eager. That was the trouble with a lot of the female Friends. They wanted to help so much they were like horses straining bare-toothed at their bits. And behind it all was the sharpest goad of all. Guilt. Because their body parts were all in running order; which was more than you could say for most of us here.

So I said, 'Fine. Just fine.' And in case they hadn't got the message, 'That's fine by me.'

We'd established that they were Friends *and* friends and Aunt Nell relaxed a bit. She was wearing a powder-blue sweater, supposed to match her eyes perhaps, and it emphasized her heavy breasts and red neck. Uncle Roger wore a tweed sports coat, grey flannels and a white shirt. He took up the bowling by producing a bag of sweets, offering me one and saying, 'Good . . . well, as one friend to two others – what d'you think of Thornton Hall?'

Aunt Nell laughed on cue and I grinned again obediently. It was so obvious they'd rehearsed at home beforehand.

'Smashing.' I looked at the sweets. 'I'm not supposed to. Extra weight you know.'

'Just this once.' They looked roguish and conspiratorial, then spoilt it all. 'We asked Doctor Beamish.'

'Thanks all the same.' I shook my head. 'We get enormous meals here.' People always want to hear what you eat as if you were some unusual animal, so I gave them a menu. 'We had soup for lunch – tomato, my favourite.

Then toad-in-the-hole. Then apple charlotte with ice-cream.'

'Sounds nice.' Uncle Roger glanced at Aunt Nell, passing the ball to her.

She said, 'And your room, Frances, dear – are you happy with your room?'

'Yes, thanks. It's a very interesting room. A funny shape – the window sticks out from the roof so there's a bit by the bed, then another bit round the corner.'

'You don't have to thank *us*, dear. I expect you mean a dormer. But those rooms are on the second floor, Frances, dear. Are you sure you can manage? Er – the wheel-chair –'

I said quickly before she could get embarrassed, 'Sure. There's a lift. Plenty of ramps.'

I could have asked them up but I'd only moved in last night and it was still not quite mine. I didn't want invaders yet. I'd already told the boss-man I'd clean it myself and I'd put some sealing tape across the door when I came down so that I'd know if anyone had been in.

Aunt Nell glanced at Uncle Roger. Their eyes nearly watered.

'Well done, lass,' said Uncle Roger.

Aunt Nell smiled. 'We're proud of you already, d'you know that?'

This because I could use a lift? I shuffled about and tried to blush and there was a long, deep silence.

Then Uncle Roger cleared his throat and said briskly, 'Well now. We've covered the place – the food and your room. What about the people here?'

Thank God he didn't say patients. Or even residents. People covered the staff as well as us and I always found the staff interesting.

I said experimentally, 'Casey's okay. Nice legs. She's got her eye on Beamish I think.'

Aunt Nell's eyebrows went up and down in bewilderment. Uncle Roger at last managed a proper grin.

'You mean Staff Nurse Casey? She's certainly gorgeous, but Doctor Beamish is a dedicated man.'

'So what? He's got eyes. She'll make him see her one of these days.'

Aunt Nell's voice almost shredded away. 'Frances, dear. Really. I don't think you should talk like that about the staff.'

Uncle Roger squeezed her powder-blue arm. 'Why not? It shows our lass takes an interest in things outside herself. She's a sharp one – only been here a day and –'

'– not the sort of thing one would wish her to . . .' Aunt Nell's protest petered out like surf in the shallows and she leaned forward again, determined to take me seriously. 'Besides Frances, dear, don't you find that kind of – er – enamelled prettiness – er – rather hard?'

I nodded, thrilled that she'd actually looked at someone and formed an opinion.

'She's tough is Casey. That's what I like about her. She isn't going to let it get her down. Plenty of pancake and eyeshadow and a few choice words –' She hadn't got a bedside manner. When I'd started yapping at her last night asking her questions, she'd told me to shut up and get to bed and I'd find out for myself in good time. I liked that because it was what she'd say to anyone whether they were paraplegic or not.

Uncle Roger entered into the spirit of the conversation, pursing his lips judiciously. 'Not the type for Doc Beamish would you say, lass?'

I nodded again. 'He needs someone like her. A protector. He's all quivery inside. Too sorry for us.' I looked away from them hoping they wouldn't think I was being personal. My eyes met those of one of the old girls from the geriatric side. Thornton Hall was like that – it contained young, old, middle-aged, everyone jumbled up just like in real life. There were even a pair of mentally deficient dogs. At least, they acted mentally deficient what with drooling and flopping about all over the place and thinking the old men's walking sticks were tree trunks. This old girl must have had new teeth fitted because she had a grin like a Jap officer in an old American War movie, and as I looked at her, she put up a quick hand and whipped out the top set. Then she gave an ecstatic sigh, smiled at me nicely, her chin jutting forward like a prize-fighter's and closed her eyes. I grinned.

Aunt Nell's hand fluttered about my arm again.

'No one could accuse you of that, Frances, dear. Self-pity is obviously not one of your sins.'

I felt like shouting at the top of my voice. How long would it be before Uncle Roger and Aunt Nell realized I was no saint? I looked her straight in the eye.

'Don't be too sure of that. Beamish's raw compassion makes it difficult for him to see *any* woman. Which makes me damned sorry for myself. I think I could fancy him.'

That did it. The blue eyes nearly fell out and the facial muscles would have snapped if they'd stretched any further.

'Frances, *dear*! You really must not talk like that!'

'Why not? Because I've got no feelings from the waist down?'

She was even more appalled. 'You know I didn't mean . . . you're only six*teen*!'

'Two years older than Juliet, I believe.'

'It's not –' The voice snapped off and began again with difficulty. '. . . I don't mean . . .' She reached for Uncle Roger. 'It was the *way* you . . . Frances, dear, you sounded almost coarse!'

As Aunt Nell said that Victorian word, I saw that Uncle Roger was laughing. It was a chink of light in a fast-dimming room.

'That's part of my trouble,' I said solemnly. 'I am coarse. It's got something to do with always wetting my knickers, I think. I have to dwell on the more basic things of life.' I smiled my specially charming smile. 'It's so difficult to know how to put it. Other than saying I could fancy Doctor Beamish myself.'

Aunt Nell smiled back forgivingly. But she obviously thought sex wasn't a suitable subject for a sixteen-year-old paraplegic because she then said brightly, 'Have you seen the games room? We understand you're very good at table tennis and billiards?'

I shook my head. 'I've not seen anything much. Last night the interview with Beamish. Then up to my room. This morning – bath – examination – lunch – you.'

'Let's take you along then, shall we?' Aunt Nell jumped up gratefully. 'It'll be fun showing you around.' She tried to get behind me and I turned my chair to face her.

'Don't push me!' I heard my voice go up a notch and brought it down. 'I can manage. I don't like to be pushed, thanks.'

Aunt Nell fell back, frustrated. Uncle Roger said easily, 'That's good. It means we can go on talking without shouting over your shoulder.'

There was more to Uncle Roger than met the eye. He pointed to double swing doors beyond the old girl with the teeth – or rather, without the teeth – and paced beside me. He was very tall but he bent his head courteously, his hands clasped behind his back. If we'd had anything to say we could have talked without difficulty. As I manoeuvred past the group of armchairs I spotted the teeth lying glisteningly on a side table. Without a thought I swept them into my tidy bag which hung from the arm of my chair and bowled straight at the doors so that they opened and immediately closed behind me. The old girl didn't see a thing. I wondered about a career in crime; who would suspect a thief in a wheel-chair?

The games room was empty so soon after lunch. It was vast. The two billiard tables and three table tennis decks were lower than usual. There was a punch ball, darts boards, quoits, even a basket-ball pitch.

Uncle Roger and Aunt Nell joined me, breathing audibly.

'It's marvellous,' I said quickly. I spun my chair around the nearest table. 'Better than anything I've seen before. Yes, it's quite a place, Thornton Hall. I'm going to like it.'

Aunt Nell bleated, 'Frances, dear, what's happening? Why did you –?'

'I'm showing off.' I laughed at them and went into reverse, spun on to the basket-ball pitch, did a figure-of-eight. 'I'm good aren't I? Some girls get biceps like wrestlers. I'm lucky.' I was proud of my arms and hands. I was wearing a tight black tee shirt with long sleeves that afternoon, and I'd done my nails a silvery pink. I could see Aunt Nell was in two minds as to whether she should be pleased I took an interest in my appearance or whether she should disapprove of anyone physically handicapped being vain enough to use nail varnish.

Uncle Roger said levelly, 'Frances. Why did you take Mrs Gorman's dental plate just now?'

So I hadn't been completely invisible. I fluttered my fingers and gasped a laugh, all feminine.

'I do things like that. I don't know why. They were there.'

Aunt Nell was bewildered, out of her depth. The other

11

girl – the one who died – was probably sad and submissive and Aunt Nell thought I'd be the same. Uncle Roger gave me a long stare, then went and fetched a couple of folding chairs, opened them and urged his wife to sit on one.

He said, 'What are you going to do with the teeth?'

'Put them back.' I stared at him. His neutral grey eyes held depths which I couldn't fathom but which gave me hope. I stopped being girlish and leaned forward slightly. 'Don't you see? I like things to happen. Not just physio and playing table tennis and people dying. Things that *I* make happen. Nothing to do with the Homes and hospitals. For instance –' It had only just occurred to me, but it became a shining certainty on the instant. '– before I leave Thornton Hall I'm going to fix things between Nurse Casey and Doc Beamish!'

They both recoiled as if from a gust of wind. Aunt Nell's mouth opened slightly but still she was speechless. Uncle Roger was the first to recover and he started to grin again.

'I see. Should be interesting.' He glanced at Aunt Nell asking for her support. She made an obvious effort to relax. He went on, giving her time. 'Somehow, Frances, the way you spoke of leaving here gave the impression you thought your stay might be short.' He raised sandy brows at me humorously. That meant they didn't know. I'd made a point before I accepted the place here that no one must know. Beamish of course. But no one else. It didn't bother me much, but it bothered everyone else like hell. They thought because my days were numbered they had to wear kid gloves and a halo when they were with me. I was grateful Beamish had kept his promise as far as Aunt Nell and Uncle Roger went – for their sakes; I couldn't imagine how they would manage otherwise.

'Could be.' I grinned at them both and was glad to see Aunt Nell's still parted lips tremble a slight response. 'I get moved on quite a bit. No one liked my record player at the last place. The one before objected to my pets.'

'Pets?' Aunt Nell was on my side now. I'd noticed how she fussed around the pair of mentally deficient dogs.

'Mice. I let them out of their cage for exercise. You should have seen how the staff jumped about.'

'But you were only a little girl then. Surely a prank like that –'

I shrugged. 'There were other things.'

Aunt Nell's imagination boggled and she sat back in her chair. Uncle Roger said rallyingly, 'Well. No one will hear your player if you're up in the dormer room. And you've got the dogs – they'll be pets enough for you I should think.'

I grinned again. 'If you could have seen them at lunch time – I'm surprised they let them within a mile of the place.'

'There you are. Thornton Hall is different. They'll put up with you.'

I began to like him. We laughed and after a bit Aunt Nell joined in. Then I said I'd give Mrs Gorman's teeth back and they trailed after me into the lounge. And there was poor old Mrs Gorman going through her tidy bag like a maniac while one of the nurses stood over her and all her neighbours gazed on with interest.

The nurse walked off in disgust as I arrived.

'I've got them!' I slewed my chair round in front of the old lady and began to search my bag. 'I'm sorry Mrs Gorman – I thought you'd be asleep for ages and I just – I just –' It sounded so feeble now, I couldn't go on.

I produced them and looked up expecting her to be all to pieces like so many old people. But she had that toothless grin on her face again and her chin jutted towards me confidentially.

'You keep 'em my love. Go on, put 'em back in that bag of yours. I hate the bleeding things and everyone says "persevere with them Mrs Gorman" – "you look years younger Mrs Gorman"!' She made a hissing sound of disgust. 'As if I want to look young and silly again. As if I can't mungle my food around quite well without them – and speak clearer too!' She closed one eye at me. 'No, you did me a good turn young lady. You keep them safe for me. If I want them, I'll know where they are.'

I looked at her with my eyes popping to beat Aunt Nell's. It was like meeting an old friend; someone who enjoyed stirring things up as much as I did myself.

Uncle Roger leaned over me, his smile fully fledged. 'The biter bit, eh, Frances Adamson?'

I began to laugh. Uncle Roger laughed. Mrs Gorman cackled. Aunt Nell looked bewildered but willing to be amused. Another old girl and two men rustled newspapers disapprovingly. The dogs lolloped over and lay on their backs, showing everything they'd got and smiling their mentally deficient smiles.

A questing nurse arrived and with a quick motion Mrs Gorman whipped the teeth from my fingers and dropped them back into my tidy bag. At last Aunt Nell giggled.

'Listen.' Uncle Roger crouched by the chair. 'Don't do anything too drastic will you? It would be nice if you could hang on here for a while.'

I could have wept. Except that I never did.

CHAPTER TWO

The sellotape was unbroken on my door. I swung it open and sat still staring at my room from the threshold. It had terrific possibilities. There's a lot to be said for functional Homes, but their big drawback is that the architects have used up all the possibilities themselves. Thornton Hall might have been very functional for Sir Richard Thornton and his horde of family and servants, but for physically handicapped people it was very non-functional. Which gave it terrific possibilities.

I left the door open and glided slowly into the tented glass of the dormer window. It was quite a big area, probably five by five, and the window came down low enough for me to see over the grounds to the new Avon bridge and the teeming motorway traffic. Directly below, the primrose yellow plastic that covered the swimming pool glinted in the setting sun, and beyond that were trees and paths and more trees around the reedy lake. Loads of it, stretching right and left. I marked various things I'd like to see as soon as possible. I was determined to explore thoroughly; make it mine.

I must begin with the room. That must be welded to me first of all so that even if I died tomorrow it would be Fran's room. Even if my mother had cared little enough to put me on the steps of the Social Security offices in Bristol without a name or pedigree or legs that worked – I was still a person. I didn't intend to go out like a guttering candle; people were going to know I'd been here. Me: Frances Adamson.

I turned slowly on my left wheel, surveying the low sloping ceiling that begged for posters, the pitted but glossy floorboards that might even be prised up to reveal secret caches. My trunk stood before the low cupboard half unpacked, Dorothy, my black rag cat, lying on top of forty pairs of knickers, my cherished half-cup bras still in their cellophane bags. As long as Dorothy had air and vision the unpacking could wait until the morning, but I had to make a start on personalizing the room before dinner.

The door blew a little further open and said 'zeek'. A pleasant nudging comment, reminding me of its solid wooden presence. I smiled at it, complimenting it for not being faced up like other less noble doors. It would take drawing pins securely and with equanimity. The door zeeked again and my smile broadened because of course it was telling me to start right here; to blazon my presence on its glowing torso.

I needed something special. I rummaged through my magazines; brochures of Canada, rail trips in Scotland, a guide to London. At last I came upon the right thing just as the dinner gong shuddered along the passage. A nosegay of flowers so intensely blue they would make Aunt Nell's eyes look albino. I cut them out carefully and stuck them on temporarily with some of that putty stuff, closed the door, re-sealed it and studied the effect. Yes, it would do. Nothing but flower pictures would go on my door. I would call my room the flower room and make sure that the smell of flowers drowned even the deodorant which was supposed to cover my wet knickers.

I grinned with satisfaction as I spun towards the lift. And it was only as I pressed the ground floor button that I realized those blue flowers were forget-me-nots. Appropriate of course, but a bit like a plea? I nearly went back and ripped them off. Then I thought if I hadn't recognized them instantly, neither would anyone else. And when they did they wouldn't connect a thing. Most people who worked in Homes were under-sensitive. They had to be, else they got raw like Doc Beamish, then they had to leave to protect themselves. That made me wonder how long I had to work on the Doc Beamish/Staff Nurse Casey romance and that got my urgency syndrome started up so I was practically fizzing as I waited for the lift doors to open and bowled myself down the ramp into the dining room. And of course I was last.

One of the helpers indicated the place I'd had at lunch time; a round table for three with two thalidomide girls, younger than me and marvellously dexterous. But armless. And how could I be proud of my arms and hands when they had none? I kept my beaming smile intact and swivelled round to Granny Gorman's side. There was no place laid but just enough room for my wheels. The old man on my left clicked with annoyance and snatched his tripod walking stick to the other side of him as if he thought I was after it. Granny didn't even notice my arrival and continued spooning soup into her toothless face with great concentration.

The helper galloped over.

'Dearie, your seat is over here. With Stella and Penny. Don't you remember?' Her voice was gay, indulgent.

I smiled winningly. 'D'you mind if I stay here? I told Mrs Gorman – promised – I would sit by her.'

'Eh?' The tortoise head turned towards me with difficulty. 'Oh, it's you is it, Miss Termagant? I wondered where you'd got to. I told that old fool Pope to leave room for you in case I needed my choppers.'

The dinner lady left us and Mr Pope clicked and fidgeted. Mrs Gorman ignored him.

'It's battered fish after. Crispy it is. Spoils if you mungle it around too long. Just put the teeth on my lap, lovey. That's it – I shan't need them for my soup but they'll be handy there.'

I placed the teeth reverently on her floral rayon dress and leaned back to include Mr Pope.

'Sorry to come between you two,' I said, mostly to him. 'But I could see you needed a chaperone and I wouldn't like you to give the place a bad name.'

Granny loved it. She cackled and spluttered something about chance being a fine thing. Mr Pope surfaced from his soup plate and looked at me.

'I'll thank you to mind your own business, young lady!' The loose skin under his chin wobbled like a turkey's. 'Why don't you sit with your own age group and make your smart–alec remarks to them?'

Granny took up the cudgels with relish.

'She's sitting here because I like her sitting here!' She leaned across me and her chin nearly stabbed his eye. 'And I like her smart–alec remarks. They're better than your silence any day. They make me feel I'm still alive. You make me feel I was buried last year!'

They tried to stare each other out in front of my face; then the helper arrived with my soup plate and cutlery. They relapsed, both breathing audibly. It had doubtless done their respirations and hearts a lot of good, that little confrontation. I felt smug.

It was gorgeous soup. The fish arrived, nestling crisply in a bed of fluffy white creamed potatoes. There were peas and diced carrots in stainless steel dishes if you wanted them. Granny fitted her teeth behind her handkerchief while I smothered my plate in tomato ketchup. We ate without conversation, appreciatively. Mr Pope scooped his fish from the batter shell, mashed it with a little of the potato and forked it slowly into his mouth. I waited until he put the fork down and drank some water.

'Don't you want your crispy outside?' I indicated the batter with a glance. 'I'll eat it for you if you like.'

He pushed his plate further from me. 'No thank you.'

'Sorry. I just thought –'

Granny saw her chance and took up arms again with alacrity.

'You want to leave it there to give the cook a guilty conscience – that's it, isn't it? You always have to leave something on your plate! Go on, let *her* have it – she knows how to enjoy her food. Go on, push it on to her plate –' she reached across with her knife and scooped the flimsy batter over with deceptive speed.

'No, really –' I didn't want to be involved in an actual hand-to-hand battle on my second day. It might well be the first black mark that would lead to expulsion. 'You leave it, Mr Pope. I didn't mean to deprive you.'

A helper's face appeared, moon-like, hovering over us from behind.

'Any difficulties, Mr Pope?' Upside-down the honeyed smile was ghoulish. 'We know about your appetite, but Cook does so hope that tonight she's tempted you to . . . why, Mr Pope!' Genuine pleasure crept into the voice. 'You've cleared your plate! Well done! Cook will be delighted. And the sweet is plain ice-cream, so that should slip down a treat.'

Mr Pope hesitated, considering spilling the beans, then accepted temporary defeat.

'I don't want any ice-cream,' he said at last like a

protest-marcher hanging on to the last shred of his banner. 'Nasty cold stuff to go to bed on.'

I turned away from him. 'Bring him a small helping,' I said quietly. 'I'll persuade him to eat it.'

Granny and I split his ice-cream between us and Granny produced a battered bar of chocolate from her tidy-bag which we crumbled over the top. He ostentatiously didn't watch us, but he didn't entirely retreat into silence. When Granny asked him if he would have just a spoonful, he sprang to the attack immediately.

'Not when it is covered in chocolate probably as old as you and even less hygienic!' he said with relish. He'd obviously spent a happy five minutes cooking up that remark and he couldn't resist smiling over it. Strangely enough, Granny liked it too and chortled as she popped the proffered spoonful into her own mouth. Then, when we'd finished, along came the cook herself to tell Mr Pope what a good clever boy he was, and while she was doing that the helper congratulated me on persuading him to eat a proper meal.

'Older people can be shy about eating in front of youngsters,' she told me, as much the amateur social worker as Aunt Nell. 'But you certainly did wonders for those two. Look at Mrs Gorman laughing.'

I looked. Granny was almost apoplectic and as I caught her eye I let the smugness dissolve into giggles. I only hoped that as well as black marks they put silver or gold ones by your name at Thornton Hall. Because I must have earned myself two or three that night.

One of the night staff greeted me gaily in the corridor.

'You're the new girl – Frances, isn't it? Where would you like to go – games room – television – reading?'

'I'd like to go outside.' I was in a good mood and I

smiled at her. 'Please call me Fran. I'm called Frances when I'm in trouble.'

'Which isn't often, I hope.' Grey eyes smiled at me sentimentally. 'I'm Nurse Bennett. Just an auxiliary really. I answer to Bennie except when Sister's in earshot.' She had a nice laugh. 'You're not actually supposed to go outside after dinner, Fran. We've cleared up and locked the main doors and we like to start the baths as soon as possible.'

'I have my bath in the morning. And I would love to see a bit of the garden.' I put everything I had into a pleading look. 'I came yesterday and I haven't had time to see outside. I really need some air.'

She capitulated without a struggle. 'Oh, all right. This way. You can go out on to the terrace and there's a ramp from there to the main path. Have you got a watch?' We synchronized watches. 'No more than half an hour, mind, otherwise you'll find yourself locked out.' She looked soppy again. 'The times I've said that to my daughter and she doesn't take a bit of notice.'

She'd got a daughter about my age; she was going to be a soft touch. I followed her into the room where I'd sat with Uncle Roger and Aunt Nell that afternoon. A series of big, old-fashioned french doors led on to the terrace, and Nurse Bennett – Bennie – opened one with a clandestine air and stood aside while I shoved my way through.

'Half an hour,' she whispered.

'Half an hour,' I agreed solemnly and trundled along the terrace without another glance at my watch.

There were masses of flowers. Honeysuckle waved its fronds over the stone balustrade, aubrietia pushed between the pot-bellied pillars, brown and yellow gallardias marched alongside the ramp, and beyond them were bushes of floribunda roses. I had scissors in my tidy bag

and I moved slowly, cutting a flower here and there so that
there were no gaps; I'd had experience of irate gardeners
before. Soon my lap was piled with flowers. I came upon
forget-me-nots growing wild behind a low box hedge and
wedged a tight bunch between the frame and canvas of my
chair. Then some giant cushions of lavender, and what
better flower than lavender for scenting a room?

The sun was gone by this time and tangled skeins of
gnats danced crazily over the dampening lawn. They
reminded me of how I felt sometimes; they were a model
of the constantly moving atom. I left the path and forced
my wheels over the resilient turf to join them. The house
looked lovely from here; the terrace floated above me and
the grey ribbon of the drive wound in a huge sweep from
the other side of the house girdling this lawn and the gnats
on its way to the Lodge and the main gates. Some of the
windows were lit and I tried to find mine but as there was
no sign of the yellow swimming pool roof, I guessed it
must be somewhere else. The sense of being on my own in
all this gracious space was exhilarating and very unusual. I
was happy and relaxed but I hadn't lost the terrific sense of
anticipation that had met me as I arrived yesterday in the
ambulance. Slowly I leaned down and began to pick the
shuttered daisies, and in the half light I made a daisy chain
and put it on my head.

How long I might have stayed there exulting, I don't
know, but just then a prosaic white ambulance revved up
the incline from the gates and began the long parabola to
the house. I watched it in the twilight and wondered
whether it contained a new person to be investigated.
Certainly the driver would see me and report my strange
presence.

With a sigh I started back to the terrace and the watching
Bennie. She smuggled me and the flowers back to my

room and brought me a selection of vases and jam-jars and a seed catalogue with some gorgeous flower pictures for Zeek, the door. She said she'd look in at ten to make sure I'd got myself into my nightie and sani-pads properly and she wouldn't be surprised if she didn't bring a nice cup of coffee and some custard cream biscuits with her.

Bennie was going to be the perfect ally. I began to sort my flowers on the table by my trunk. Dorothy watched me from her button eyes and looked very contented as the lavender, honeysuckle, rose and montbretia smell permeated the room.

'I've got to finish unpacking that trunk,' I told her severely. 'And there're all these flowers. And the door. They won't let me keep my room private if I can't sort it out by tomorrow!'

Dorothy grinned at me. She didn't care about the chores. The night was long and neither of us were sleepy and the possibilities of Thornton Hall were endless.

CHAPTER THREE

At midnight the phone burped discreetly like internal phones do. Granny Gorman's voice rasped across the line.

''Tisn't no good you trying to say anything, Miss Termagant. I can't hear on these things. But so long as you're not asleep, come on down and get my choppers. You were in such a darned hurry to leave the dining room I didn't have time to give them to you.'

I hadn't actually fancied the idea of handling them directly after use; anyway I had assumed that particular joke had come to an end.

'Can't hear you,' Granny bawled in my ear. 'I've cleaned 'em up nicely and they're here waiting. And I've found some more chocolate in my tidy bag.'

The phone clicked horribly as she fumbled it back down. I could imagine her, chin like Punch's, sitting up in bed grinning at the carrot she'd offered me. Of course I was going. Nothing to do with the teeth or chocolate. I'd been waiting for an excuse like this.

The corridor was dimly lit and spooky with its dark oak and the emptiness like a presence. I thumbed my nose at it and paused to stare at Zeek. Already he was beautiful with a line of flower pictures extending from handle level to floor. I'd have to get someone to do the top half for me. Bennie probably.

There were other doors on my corridor but none of them had numbers on so they must be cupboards or extra bathrooms or something. I wondered whether they'd given me an isolated room as a treat or to segregate me from the others. Whatever the reason it *was* a treat.

I was on the ground floor before I realized I didn't know Granny's room number. I paused, nibbling my lip. There would be a list of names and corresponding room numbers somewhere near the kitchen probably in case anyone needed meals served in bed. It was my only hope. I bowled on towards the dining room, my wheels soundless on the wide oak boards, my ears singing with the effort to hear anyone before they heard me. Just beyond the double doors, which I remembered concertina'd into the dining room, there was a narrow, dark passage turning to the left; a light over the door at the end. It was the kitchen, a new one doubtless made from the old morning room or something. On a bank of modern hobs a kettle and pan of milk were steaming gently. The staff were going to have their midnight drink very soon.

I looked around. There was a notice board with about a million lists on it. Menus, duty rotas, individual diet sheets – Mr Pope was a hiatus hernia so maybe he wasn't such a fusspot after all – and at the top almost out of my vision, two dozen neatly typed names aligned to neatly typed numbers. On the end in scribbly writing were two extra names. Frances Adamson, number seventy-eight, and right at the very bottom, Lucas Hawkins, number five. Was he the new arrival in the ambulance that night? I zipped on up the list and found Granny next to Stella Graves. Number eleven. Legs eleven. I muttered it in my mind though it was unforgettable anyway, then I backed off hastily, did a three-point turn by the array of sinks, and

25

shot back down the little passage and into the big shadowy hall where at least I could pretend I was looking for Bennie instead of sneaking food.

No one was about. In view of the kettle and milk saucepan it was surprising until I found room number five. Then a soothing voice from behind the door told me that Bennie had been waylaid on her way to make the hot drinks.

'Now . . . don't take on so, my love. Why don't you let me get you a nice cup of coffee and take two more of your pain killers and –?'

A savage voice interrupted her. 'Because I can't live on bloody pain killers! Because I'm sick of being doped up to the eyeballs!'

I stopped and eavesdropped unashamedly. The voice was young and it hadn't occurred to me that someone called Lucas Hawkins could be under forty.

Bennie was almost weeping. 'I understand, my dear – of course I do – but why go without them *now*? At night, when you're alone? Tomorrow when you're with the others –'

'I'm never with anyone else – it's just me and this –' I wondered where he was pointing. Legs? Arms? Or just the pain?

Bennie said, 'You've come here so that you won't be *able* to shut yourself away like that. It's wrong. There are others here –'

'Other cripples d'you mean? Like me, d'you mean? So that I won't feel odd man out, d'you mean?' The laugh was unpleasant. 'That really is funny. Like blind schools. Or places for the deaf and dumb. In the end no one sees, speaks or hears. Great. Just great.'

'Don't be so bitter, my dear –' Casey could have dealt with him. She'd have told him to shut up. Bennie didn't

26

know what to say. 'It's not like that. There are young people – and elderly –'

'Great again. I just stay on till I'm geriatric, is that it?'

Bennie changed her tactics. 'Look. I'm going to get you a nice hot drink and two pain killers. No, don't argue, otherwise I'll also get Doctor Beamish and heaven knows he needs his rest.' She went on but I didn't wait for the rest. Poor old Bennie, if she found me out of bed now she really would burst into tears.

I got along to legs eleven all right and Granny Gorman wasn't a bit surprised to see me.

'Come on in, Miss Termagant,' she called to my sur-reptitious knock. ''Tisn't locked.' I opened the door and shoved myself in. She was sitting in bed, the teeth huge and hideous on the bed table. 'What's the good of locking when they've got a master key anyway?' Her nightie was like a shroud and her hair fell wispily around her face. No wonder Lucas Hawkins wasn't mad on being associated with geriatrics. I pulled out a handful of tissues from her box and buried the teeth in them and stuck the whole lot in my tidy bag. I'd completely gone off the idea of being Keeper of the Teeth.

She was rummaging with silver paper around a lump of chocolate and she stopped suddenly and looked at me with her beady eyes.

'What's the matter, Miss Termagant – you're quiet.'

I was going to say I couldn't speak till I'd been sustained with chocolate, but meeting that all-knowing gaze, I asked, 'Don't you mind?'

'Mind?' The chin tucked itself in and she looked slightly less evil. 'Being old? Or having to depend on things like false teeth?'

I shrugged and wished I hadn't asked such a damned silly question.

She grinned again. 'Of course I mind. I'm still me inside this lot you know.' She stabbed at her chest with an arthritic finger. 'Still May Gorman who could lead the chaps a fair dance . . .' She stopped herself. 'Daft, isn't it? I feel the same inside. Then I catch sight of myself in a mirror.' She cackled. 'Then for a bit my inside matches my outside.'

I said bleakly, 'Then I suppose you look at some of the others – the younger ones – and you think to yourself – well, at least I had my day. Is that how you cheer yourself up?'

Her hairless brows drew together. 'Doesn't work like that. They make me feel worse. The way they manage – their whole aim in life is to manage. Social training or whatever the good doctor calls it. Have you seen that little Davis girl? No arms and she eats her meals better than old Pope!'

'I've seen her.' I wanted to wail a reminder that I had no legs.

A wheezy laugh blew the inverted lips out full-size.

'No. Tell you what cheers me up. When a cheeky young miss comes along and whips my choppers for a joke. They don't make her feel sick – I don't make her feel sick. She talks to me as if she can still see May Gorman behind this lot –' another jab at her chest, '– she lets me help her stir things up a bit. That's what cheers me up!'

I stared at her for a long time. I wasn't sure whether I'd seen May Gorman or not, but she'd seen Frances Adamson. Not a paraplegic Frances Adamson.

I said slowly, 'I've got wild plans for fixing up Staff Nurse Casey with Doctor Beamish.'

She crowed with delight and I thought we were about to lay full-scale plans together. Then she sobered suddenly and jutted her chin at me.

'Off to bed Miss Termagant! Go on – take your chocolate and get yourself off. You'll be all eyes and no face
tomorrow.'

When I was a kid there was a zoo outing and a nine-year-
old boy had pointed to the marmosets and yelled, 'Look –
they're like Frannie! Frannie looks like a monkey!' All eyes
and no face.

I bit into the chocolate and said fearfully, 'You don't
think I look like a monkey do you, Granny?'

All the lines in her face sagged into quietness and she
looked as old as the hills.

'I think you're beautiful,' she said slowly with not a
harsh note in her voice. Then the lines leapt up and she was
Mrs Mephistopheles again. 'But you act like a monkey.
That's for sure. You certainly act like a monkey!'

I left her and made cautiously for the lift. The ramp was
a devil going back, I ought to have taken a run at it but I
was so darned tired all of a sudden. It was good to push up
the arm of my chair and roll into the turned-down bed next
to Dorothy. The sheets smelled of lavender and the other
flowers smiled at me from all around the room. I settled
back on to the high pillows with a sigh of content. Then I
remembered Lucas Hawkins.

I lay there, thinking for a bit, not switching off the light.

Then I picked up the phone and pressed button number
five.

A long burr sounded in my ear. Pause. Another burr.
How many before I concluded he was asleep? There was a
click.

A voice said wearily, 'You don't have to worry. I'm
okay. Just leave me alone.'

I said, 'With pleasure. Tell me this first, Hawkins. Did
you take the pain killers?'

'Who is that?'

'Did you take the pain killers?'

'I thought the one thing I'd get in this dead-end hole was privacy. Now I find there's some kind of Big Brother system working –'

'Cut the drivel, Hawkins. Did you take the damn-and-blasted pain killers?'

'No.' There was surprise in the monosyllable.

'Why not?'

'I don't have to tell you or anyone else that. Whoever you are.' But he didn't put the phone down.

'Not anyone else. No. But me. Yes. Why didn't you take 'em?'

'Because I don't want to join the clan. Okay? I don't want to pretend I can be just as good as I was before. Now will you get off this phone and leave me strictly alone?'

'Sure. Like I said, with pleasure. One thing before I go, Hawkins. You did the right thing about the pain killers. Wrong motive though.'

'Hey?'

'You want to die, right? Well, let me tell you, boy. When you're hurting somewhere, you know for sure you're alive.'

I put the phone down gently without saying good night and lay holding Dorothy and staring at the ceiling for a while before I put out my light.

CHAPTER FOUR

Casey rolled my wet draw-sheet into the laundry basket, re-made my bed, bathed and dried me and wheeled me back to my room – all in total silence.

'You're not much on the small talk are you?' I inquired pleasantly as I rummaged for one of my new bras in the half-empty trunk.

'I've got plenty to say to you my girl when you're dressed,' Casey came back, grimly putting my jeans and black tee shirt on the bed and kneeling to force socks on to the legs which are attached to my torso for some reason. 'As for small talk. I didn't think you needed it.'

'I don't.' I looked down at her carefully riotous blonde hair beneath the cap and the red nurse's hands oddly at variance with her Marilyn Monroe figure and face. 'Not the usual kind anyway. I'd like to know something about the new arrival in number five. And I'd also like to know whether Doctor Beamish is married. Plus – who is Uncle Roger and Aunt Nell's adopted nephew.'

She took it all without batting an eyelid. She stood up, whipped the bra out of its cellophane and snapped, 'Get on with it. You'll be late for breakfast and I've got other people to –'

'You don't have to tell me. I'll find out anyway.'

She said woodenly, 'Doctor Beamish is unmarried. I don't know anything about number five. He came in after

I'd gone off duty last night. And Mr and Mrs Parrish regularly visit Timmy Royston who is now in the sanatorium.'

'Thanks. Concisely put. I think I'll visit the sanatorium this morning and get Timmy's opinion on Aunt Nell's hot flushes.'

'I don't think you will.'

She said it flatly as she passed me my jeans and stood aside watching me crouch and fumble into them. I knew what she meant. Uncle Roger and Aunt Nell would be 'adopting' a new nephew any day now. I hesitated only a moment. Death is merciful in places like Thornton Hall and I accepted it most of the time, but it *was* depressing to find that two places were vacated so quickly. I tugged my jeans fiercely upward and began to rock from side to side to get them up to my waist.

'The new arrival is rather premature, isn't he?' I asked. After all, if Timmy Royston knew about him, it couldn't cheer him up much.

She laid out my brush and comb and tidied the dressing table with a few swift efficient movements that were a pleasure to see.

'Not very,' she said in the same expressionless voice. Then she went to the door and picked up the laundry basket. 'Now it's my turn. You've been here three days, Frances, and I already know of three . . . mistakes . . . you've made.'

'Mistakes?' I opened my eyes very wide knowing darn well I looked like an orphaned marmoset.

'You have acquired a set of false teeth which are not yours. You have eaten too many sweet things when you know you are on a regulated diet. And you have been outside after hours.'

My marmoset expression disappeared in horrified incredulity at the treachery of the two people I'd counted as friends.

'Tittle-tattle —' I spluttered. 'You've been listening to tittle-tattle without giving me a chance to defend myself!'

She smiled grimly. How did anyone like Marilyn Monroe manage to smile grimly.

'Not so fast, Frances. You threw a bundle of tissues into the waste bin just now. I heard them clunk and fished them out. Did you forget you'd wrapped a set of dentures in them?' She held them up triumphantly. One to Casey. 'And certainly I listen when Nurse Bennett tells me Mr Pope cannot sleep because he is hungry. And when she refused him a hot drink, he had to tell her about missing half his dinner. You see, Frances, he has a hiatus hernia and —'

'*I* know,' I said impatiently, scoring her another point for that. 'And then poor old Bennie's conscience grew heavy so she had to mention to you that she'd let me out into the garden when she shouldn't have done.'

Casey raised swallow-tail brows. 'Not at all. You're jumping to conclusions again, Frances. Look around you and use your brains. When I left you yesterday afternoon, this room was empty of flowers. Now it is full. Also you have not finished unpacking.'

I took a deep breath. Ten out of ten to Casey.

'Listen. I can explain everything. I'm not some kind of klepto-nut. Give me the teeth and I'll return them. It was a joke — just a joke. And the pudding last night — another joke.' I wondered what would happen if she knew about Granny's crumbly chocolate. 'Honestly. It was just that Mr Pope was being bloody-minded about his food. He wouldn't have had the ice-cream anyway so I thought . . . oh Casey, it wasn't *important*.'

'It would be if it became a regular habit.' She didn't give

me the teeth. They looked obscene nestling in the palm of her hand. 'And what about stripping the garden of flowers?'

'Stripping the . . .' I closed my mouth and swallowed. 'Listen. If you can find one place – one solitary place – bare of flowers in that garden, I'll give you first prize. Okay – so I sinned. I went out after the doors had been locked. But there are enough flowers in that garden to fill every room in Thornton Hall and then some over. And please forget what I said about Bennie,' I concluded swiftly.

She leaned over to my dressing table, took some tissues, re-wrapped Granny's dentures and dropped them in her pocket. Then she said, 'You make it sound very light-hearted, Frances. Maybe it is. But in a place like this we make rules for very good reasons. And our main reason is self-discipline.' She swept me with her cool blue eyes and I was conscious that I hadn't buttoned my flies yet, my shirt was in a bunch over the new bra and my hair uncombed. 'I suggest after breakfast you come back here and see to your room. That is if you still wish it to be private. If you can't cope, I'll get you some help.'

'I can cope,' I said fiercely. 'They promised me I could say myself when the cleaners could come in.'

'You have to *show* us you can cope,' she said, as if I hadn't spoken. 'And you won't have long because you're due in the physio room at ten sharp. And after that it's OT until lunch.'

Occupational therapy. Dreary, dreary.

'What's the good of having a swimming pool and a garden and a games room if they make you do OT all the time?' I whined.

'Shut up and get cracking,' she returned. And left.

I followed her to the door, tugged Zeek open and yelled

34

down the corridor, 'Why don't you go and tell Doc Beamish about my "mistakes"?'

She didn't even look back. 'It would be a chance for you two to get together!' I was provoked and childish. 'He might not stay unmarried for long! He might not stay *here* for long! Gather ye rosebuds while ye may. Grab your opportunities as they arise –' The lift doors swished shut and she was gone. I put my head on Zeek's smooth chest and knew I'd been cheap. My self-respect was in the dust.

Granny wasn't at breakfast. I ate with Stella Graves and Penny Davis. They didn't know anything about Lucas Hawkins. They couldn't talk about anything except O levels, which they were in the midst of doing. They had history all that afternoon and they recited the 1832 Reform Act like a catechism while they managed their cornflakes and scrambled egg with an adroitness that was horribly fascinating. I got back to my room as quickly as I could and began to put my stuff away in earnest. Dorothy watched me smugly, saying, 'I told you this would happen.' Even Zeek groaned approval when I left to go to physio and sealed him carefully against all intruders.

Miss Hamlin, the physio lady, was nice. They always are. She gave me rolling exercises – I hadn't done those before – and then five minutes in the sculling machine. As I pulled the oars, my legs pumped back and forth. Didn't do anything for them, but was supposed to keep the circulation going round the rest of me. It was fun. There was a kid there, a boy of about seven, having massage. He kept grinning at me. I asked him how many people there were at Thornton Hall and he said fifteen. That meant I'd still got at least six to meet, not counting Lucas Hawkins and Timmy Royston.

He said, 'We're in sort of threes. There's me and Timmy

and Rosie. Then there's you and Stella and Penny. Then there's Henry and Mr McGhie and Mrs Tirrell. Then there's Mr Pope and Mrs Gorman and Mrs Jarrett. I'm Dennis Makepeace.'

'Dennis the menace,' I panted, tugging at the oars and watching my legs pump up and down, up and down. 'That makes twelve. Who are the last three?'

He looked nonplussed. 'No one else. Twelve then. I'm not good at maths.'

'No.' That made Lucas Hawkins the thirteenth. 'I'm not much better myself. I wonder if I can guess how old you are. Umm. Thirty-two and a half. Maybe thirty-three next August.'

Dennis shook like a jelly beneath Miss Hamlin's capable hands.

'Eight and three-quarters,' he crowed. 'How old are you?'

I stopped rowing, picked up my towel delicately and mopped myself.

'Two years older than Juliet when she met Romeo,' I told him gravely.

'You're nuts,' he giggled. 'Are you going to school now?'

Miss Hamlin came over and lifted me into my chair.

'Frances is going to have a chat with Doctor Beamish now, Dennis,' she said, smiling. 'You'll see her later.' She turned to me. 'Do you know your way?'

I nodded vigorously. I didn't, but I could find out. I glanced fairly coldly at Dennis Makepeace.

'Didn't you hear me say I was sixteen?' I asked. 'I gave up school last Christmas.'

Miss Hamlin said firmly for his benefit, 'Frances will be in OT while you're having your lessons, young man. We don't waste our time at Thornton Hall, school or no school!' If she thought that was one in the eye for me, she was wrong. That is one thing I have never done. Wasted my time.

Doc Beamish was painfully thin, his eyes were coal-black buttons sunk deep into a face that seemed all long jawbone and thin curly mouth. His desk looked like a stall at a jumble sale, and his wiry hair stood on end where he combed it with his fingers. He certainly needed Casey.

He smiled warmly and shook my hand.

'Hullo again, Frances. I'm sorry I didn't get around to seeing you yesterday. How are you settling in?'

'Fine. Actually, I don't have to see a doctor every day. You checked me on arrival.'

'Oh, I know you're as strong as a horse and very independent.' His smile changed to a grin. 'I don't want to see you as a doctor. Just as another member of the family.'

'Well, hi there, Brother Beamish,' I ventured. 'How were *you* yesterday?'

His black eyes deliberately showed no surprise.

'Snowed under with paper work which I hate.' He drew his chair from behind the desk and straddled it in front of me. 'More details from you please, Frances. How are you managing in that room on the top? Would you prefer something more accessible?'

'I love it up there. The whole floor to myself.'

'Actually the staff are always up there in the night for clean linen and things. Not so private as you might think.'

'You know what I mean. I've called my door Zeek and I'm covering him with flowers. Is that okay?' Nothing like going straight to the top for permissions and things.

He was pleased. 'Go to it, Frances. That room is yours. Full stop.'

He should grin more often, he had lovely teeth. I tried

hard to look demure. 'Don't call me Frances. That's for when I'm on the mat. Fran. Call me Fran.'

'Okay, Fran. Now what about the others? I know you didn't want formal introductions all round but I hope you're getting to know the people outside your age group.'

'I know Granny Gorman quite well. Mr Pope a bit. Dennis Makepeace. I know Nurse Bennett pretty well, too. And Casey of course.'

'Casey?'

'Staff Nurse Casey. The gorgeous one. She looks like Marilyn Monroe.'

'We've got a nurse who looks like Marilyn Monroe? You must be joking, Fran.'

'I'm not. Your trouble is, you don't see anyone unless they're in wheel-chairs or on the physio couch. You should look at Casey. She's really something.'

He refused to be impressed. 'Penny and Stella are pretty stunning too, don't you think?' He meant it. He really meant it.

I nodded soberly. I knew they were attractive girls but my mind wouldn't get past those frightful hands fastened almost straight on to their shoulders. 'Clever with it too. They're in the middle of O levels. It was the 1832 Reform Act before breakfast.'

He laughed through his nose. Not much of a laugh but he was probably out of practice.

'When I read your file I knew you were a screwball, Fran. I think we might be glad of you.'

I said vigorously, 'Glad of me? Christ, you *need* me!'

This time his laugh was more than a snort and I wheeled myself to the door before it went to my head.

'Hey, have we finished talking?' he asked, hands on the back of his chair, chin on hands. 'I was going to suggest you had a go at some O levels yourself next year. Or a shorthand-typing course.'

Was he trying to tell me something? That I'd got a year? Even two? I opened the door and frowned heavily. 'You haven't been listening to me. I'm far too busy just now for anything like that.'

He laughed again. 'I'll let you off for a while, then. But you'll have to do OT, Fran.'

Thank God he let it go. I didn't want to have to come into the open and inform him that even if I had as long as three years he must be bonkers if he thought I'd waste that time at a school desk!

I pulled a ghastly face. 'Why? If I'm skidding around the place looking happy I'm a great advertisement.'

'You can still skid, in between OT sessions.'

'And physio. And baths. And meals.' I moved my head from side to side in a gorgeous Jewish way I'd cultivated after I saw *Fiddler on the Roof*. 'I should be so lucky.'

He kept laughing.

I said severely, 'Do one thing for me, Brother Beamish, will you?'

'What's that?'

'Take a look at Casey next time your paths cross.'

He shook his head despairingly. 'All right, all right.'

'A good look,' I persisted.

'Get out!' he ordered.

I bet he hadn't said that to anyone in a wheel-chair before. It made me feel great. I trundled down the corridor towards the OT room with an idiotic smile all over my face. I'd got back my self-respect all right.

That night I dialled five at just past midnight. It rang once.

He said, 'Who the hell are you? Do you make a habit of

ringing people up in the night when they're getting some sleep?'

'No. I didn't want to disappoint you. Had some pain killers today?'

'Yes.'

'Good. I knew you'd see sense.'

His blood pressure built up along the wire. 'I thought you congratulated me last night for not taking the blasted things!'

I said piously, 'You don't take 'em and you know you're still here. Then you take 'em to make here bearable.'

'You've got an answer for everything, Miss Clever Clogs. So . . . what's your name?'

'Nothing,' I came back as obscurely as possible. 'Don't put the phone down. I've something to say. I need help.'

'Is that possible?'

'Sure. Not even God can manage without help. Listen. There's a nurse here. Interested in Doc Beamish. She'd be great for him. What do I do?'

There was a long pause. He said quietly, 'You're a nurse. Match-making. Christ.'

Before I could put him wise he replaced the receiver at his end with a gentleness that had finality about it.

CHAPTER FIVE

Mrs Pountney – head Occupational Therapist – suggested that as I did not seem to be able to knit like Granny Gorman, or do petit point like Mrs Tirrell, or make stools like Henry, I might like to make a tour of the rooms and see what they had to offer. She came with me and it was all a nice surprise. There was a potter's wheel, painting equipment of all kinds, a spinning wheel and loom – things like that. Best of all, the sports room and swimming pool were under her wing and as the weather was so marvellous, I decided that swimming was what I wanted to do during my OT sessions. She smiled and agreed, probably thinking I'd soon get fed up with the chore of changing and drying and so on.

Most of the kids swam or spent a lot of time splashing. Dennis Makepeace, Penny, Stella, a tiny spinal bifida called Rosie Jimpson, besides two or three kids from local schools who were doing projects about those 'less fortunate than themselves', used the pool daily. But they had lessons as well, so a lot of the time I had it all to myself. It was marvellous. Water is the great equalizer. When Doc Beamish dived in one day we moved together unhampered by wheel-chairs and I knew my legs trailing behind me were no longer heavy and ugly. My beautiful arms and hands were so strong; I reached forward and pulled the water towards me; went under; came up; turned my head to smile at him delightedly.

He watched me pull myself on to the rubber raft.

'What's up?' I spluttered, hoping to God I wasn't obviously wetting myself.

He steadied the raft.

'It occurred to me then. The way you swam and pulled yourself up and rolled over. That's how mermaids must get on to flat rocks when they want to sun themselves.'

Now I ask you. Has any girl, whole or not, had a better compliment than that? I looked down at my legs. I didn't hate them, because they were like a mermaid's tail; that was the first time I'd looked at my legs and not hated them.

But what to say to Beamish? It had to be something to show my appreciation; my grand acceptance of his compliment. So, of course, naturally, I giggled.

However, by the time Casey peeled off my swimsuit and chucked a rough towel at me, I was feeling so smug it was sickening.

'You'd better watch out,' I told her severely when she bent to rub at my feet. 'The way things are going I'm getting ahead of you with Beamish.'

She said, 'Rub your hair for Pete's sake. And Mr Ottwell says he's put fresh flowers for you in the glass house.'

'Listen, I like to pick my own flowers,' I protested. Mr Ottwell was the gardener and had been grudgingly co-operative about my daily flower picking.

She shrugged and watched me towel and fix my bra. It took me ages but she let me do it and showed no impatience.

I said, 'Don't you want to know how?'

'How what?' There was humorous resignation in her voice. She bent to pull on my socks.

'How I'm getting ahead of you with Brother Beamish. He's looking at me. Seeing me.'

She went still and in spite of my bravado I felt quaky. You can only take the *enfant-terrible* bit so far.

At last she stood up briskly, one sock still in her hand.

'You're quite capable of putting that on yourself,' she said and her eyes were as hard as nails. 'I've got other work to do. And don't make the mistake of thinking I'm in your league where scheming is concerned, Fran, will you?'

She was gone with a swish of skirt. I struggled with that sock for ten whole minutes and then it wasn't on properly. And I began to wonder whether Casey's inside was as hard as her outside. But then when I trundled into the glass house to see Mr Ottwell, he said, 'Your nurse just bin in 'ere and says you wants to pick your own flowers. So I took them others in for the house. All I ask is – leave the dahlias alone and go sparing on the asters.'

'Yippee!' I turned my chair round on the spot and Mr Ottwell grabbed a teetering flower pot and looked frightened to death. 'Thank you – thank you – thank you! I'll stick to moon daisies and lavender, okay?' I spun myself again. 'D'you know what? She's full of love that woman! And d'you know what else . . . she *was* jealous! Just for a minute – she was really and truly jealous! As if I was a proper . . . a proper . . . *rival*!'

Ottwell looked sour. 'I don't know what you're on about, but if you're going to twirl that ruddy chair again, go outside to do it. It'll make my tomatoes giddy, that will.'

He pushed me outside and went back grumbling. But he knew as well as I did, that tomatoes thrive on twirling wheel-chairs.

It was Sunday again and my euphoria all gone. Aunt Nell and Uncle Roger took it in turns to play me at table tennis. They'd wanted to take me out in the car and I'd said no. I don't know why. The summer sky had turned a copper colour that morning and the air felt prickly on my skin. I wore a halter top and a long seersucker skirt and because of the thinness of it I thought I could smell myself. Casey, who would have told me not to be so stupid, had a day off and her relief was a tall, angular woman who believed my fretful complaints and larded the deodorant talc on, so that by lunch time it was a thick paste beneath my rubber pants.

Aunt Nell was disappointed at me turning down her suggestion.

'We were looking forward to showing you the house,' she said. 'There's a nice view of the sea from the sitting room.'

'I don't call the Bristol Channel the sea,' I said rudely.

Aunt Nell subsided, but Uncle Roger said equably, 'Water then. It has boats on it, you know. The occasional skier. Children at its edge. And it would be cool on a day like this.'

I said contrarily, 'I'm not a bit hot. Let's play table tennis. It's so boring just sitting talking.'

So we played and I beat them both. That was possible with Aunt Nell who was top heavy, but not with Uncle Roger. I was really annoyed with him for letting me win.

Aunt Nell panted exaggeratedly and said, 'Can we go and sit outside, Fran? It's rather close indoors, don't you think?'

'Okay.' I bowled ahead of them and said over my shoulder, 'I was hoping to take you upstairs to see my room but if you'd rather go outside that's okay.'

Aunt Nell dithered about on the terrace. 'Fran. How

perfectly sweet of you. What shall we do, Roger? We could talk just as easily upstairs.'

Was Uncle Roger getting at me when he said firmly, 'There's plenty of time for Fran to see our house and for us to see her room. Let's make the most of the grounds while we can.' I felt him take the handle of my chair and try as I would I couldn't outstrip him. I relapsed sulkily and let them walk me down to the big horseshoe-shaped lawn where I'd got my first flowers. They pushed me into the shade of an aspen and sat on the grass in front of me. Uncle Roger folded himself fairly neatly in the middle. Aunt Nell got down in lumbering stages like a camel. They looked portentous.

I decided immediately on the disarming approach.

'Look. I'm sorry. I know I'm being beastly and I'm sorry. It's something to do with the drugs. Every so often they have to cut them down before I blow my mind and then I get irritable and –' I recalled with exquisite clearness how exciting every new day had been last week and the thought that it was probably just the effect of the drugs made me want to cry. I finished desolately, 'I suppose this is the real me. I'm dreary and cross. I should be doing something constructive like Penny and Stella instead of bumming around kidding myself I can make life happen.' Aunt Nell was rearing up on her knees preparatory to taking me in her arms. I waved her down. 'Please don't. I'll only be rude again and upset you.' A large tear rolled down my nose and plopped off the end doubtless giving the impression of snot. 'You're such good people. But you see I've always been surrounded by good people. So I can't help inclining towards the others a little bit. Granny Gorman and Casey . . . not that they're evil or anything, but they've got a pretty good veneer. You can bang on it and it doesn't crack. Not often anyway. But you . . . when

I'm horrid to you, I know it hurts you and sometimes that gives me a kick . . . oh God, I must be a bloody sadist or something!' And I howled into the neck of my halter.

They were marvellous. They didn't say a word but they made noises and Uncle Roger's big hanky was wielded to good purpose and when I surfaced five minutes later, they each had a hand on my feet. They knew I couldn't feel that.

'I'm sorry,' I muttered.

Uncle Roger took over. 'Let's forget it, Fran. We understand each other a little better perhaps, and that can only be good.' He grinned. 'Just overlook it when we drive you mad, will you? And any time you want to bite our heads off . . . go ahead. That's what we're here for.' Didn't he realize how maddening *that* was, for a start? I swallowed but my frustration was still there. He lost the grin and went on ominously, 'Actually we do want to talk to you rather seriously. That's why we thought of taking you back home with us. Putting Thornton Hall at a distance. Seeing it in perspective as it were.'

I forgot my misery in a little nudge of pure fear. Were they going to break it to me that I'd got the sack? I couldn't bear to leave here.

'It's about the rules, isn't it?' I gulped. 'Self-discipline and all that?'

Aunt Nell actually smiled. So did Uncle Roger.

'Nothing like that, Fran. Quite the opposite.' He settled himself in a new position, legs crossed, arms clasping knees. 'First of all, you'll be sorry to hear that little Timmy Royston died yesterday.'

The way he said it. Passing regret. Would he talk like that when . . . if . . . it happened to me? Then I looked at Aunt Nell and saw her blue eyes were full of pain and her mouth thin and haggard.

46

Uncle Roger saw my glance and said matter-of-factly, 'Your Aunt Nell was with him.'

Unexpectedly I liked the way he gave me Aunt Nell. Your Aunt Nell. The ever-anxious eyes, the cumbersome figure, they were valuable because they were mine. After all, she was just as a mother should be. She was made for motherhood and to all intents and purposes I had no mother. I forced myself to reach down and touch her shoulder, and thank goodness she didn't even look at me, just bowed her head and stared down at the daisies she and Uncle Roger were busily crushing.

He continued levelly, 'Things have to go on, Fran. Our new "nephew" is called Lucas Hawkins. He's eighteen. Accident on his motor bike. Lost both legs.' He tried to make it sound clinical. 'His parents are banking on Thornton Hall.'

Lucas Hawkins was my secret. I wasn't keen on him being put under the microscope like this. And I was less keen on what was revealed there.

I said, 'I don't get it. He can learn to walk on tin legs, can't he? I thought this was a residential place. And if he's got parents why are you adopting him?'

Aunt Nell burst out, 'That's what's so awful, Frances, dear. He won't see them – won't see any of his relatives. It's all wrong – he's retreated right into himself.'

So . . . he had been all right, this Lucas Hawkins. Walking about, playing football, riding a motor bike. He hadn't been born without working legs . . . I could see it made it worse for him, but I couldn't forget the cool contempt in his voice the last time he'd spoken on the phone. The way he'd made me feel small and petty.

I said stubbornly, 'I still don't see why he's here. We're all congenital and we're here for always. It *is* our home.'

Uncle Roger put his chin on his knees. 'His people are very rich, Fran. They heard about Thornton Hall and the work Doctor Beamish does. As I said before, it's their last hope.'

Another silence while I digested this. Rich. Rich and spoiled. Speeding on a motor bike bought for him out-right.

I said, 'But they can't buy him new legs, huh?'

Aunt Nell pleaded. 'Frances. Dear. That isn't what they wanted when they thought of Thornton Hall. They wanted peace of mind for him. Acceptance of his dis-ability.'

Uncle Roger said wryly, 'It hasn't worked. He won't move from his room.'

'Stalemate,' I suggested.

'Exactly.' His grey eyes weren't so wishy-washy after all. They were very clear. 'That's where you come in, Fran.'

'Me?' Wasn't it just what I'd wanted? Hadn't I already tried to muscle in anyway? 'Not likely. Not pygmalion likely in fact.'

'Frances. *Dear* –'

'You're in the same age group,' Uncle Roger went on as if neither of us had spoken. 'In many ways you're older than he is. And he could never suspect you of pitying him – condescending to him. You could get him interested again.'

Yet another silence while I digested this too.

I said slowly, 'How could I interest him, Uncle Roger?'

He said lightly, 'Come on, Fran, that's obvious. You can interest him just as any young woman might interest a young man.'

The excitement was back. Without drugs and under that heavy copper sky, it was there again. I wanted to giggle; be coy; ask him to enlarge. I took a grip on myself and decided to be outraged.

'Do you mean I've got to *seduce* him? Don't you think that's tasteless to say the least? A paraplegic going all out for –'

Aunt Nell interrupted with a moan of physical pain. 'Frances, dear, you know we don't mean any such thing.'

Uncle Roger spoke judiciously with a twinkle in his voice.

'Face up to it, dear.' He knew I was sending them up, and he was playing my game. 'In a way that's exactly what we are asking. The strongest human urge next to hunger, is sex. And we're asking Fran to use this –'

Aunt Nell's expression was beseeching. 'Stop, Roger! I can't bear it. This is wrong. We shouldn't have listened to Doctor Beamish – we simply cannot ask Fran –'

'Doctor Beamish?' I was on to it; a cat on a mouse. 'Do you mean to tell me Brother Beamish suggested this piece of skulduggery?'

Uncle Roger knelt up suddenly. 'Not quite like that, Fran. But he did think you might be able to bring Lucas out of his hole. However, until he decides to emerge from his room, the idea is hypothetical. Let's forget it. I suggest we get permission for you to stay out late. Come on – come to our place. I want to show you the sea.'

He was crafty, was Uncle Roger. He'd cut the conversation short at a point where he knew I'd do nothing but think about it. But I played him at his own game anyway.

'Okay. On second thought I'd like that. It's getting close here.'

Uncle Roger grinned, remembering I'd denied the heat only half an hour ago. But Aunt Nell was ingenuously thrilled. She galloped over the lawn to see Beamish and collect my cardigan. She was a bit like our two daft dogs.

Honest and straightforward and imagining everyone else was the same.

I said abruptly over my shoulder to Uncle Roger, 'She must be tired. Up all last night like that.'

He said, 'She never gets tired. Not Nell.'

I watched her broad rear as it went up the ramp to the terrace. She was made for motherhood. I would have to watch I didn't get to rely on her too much.

It rained when we got to Clevedon and I watched the storm from their window on the Victorian front as it whipped the sea into waves, then a heavy spewing mass. Everything was grey. The sea, the houses, the sky, the broken pier. The string of fairy lights above the railings was tossed back and forth like a skipping rope and as it grew darker there was a dull red glow on the horizon that was the blast furnaces over in Wales.

It excited me to near fever pitch. I wanted to be one with the storm. I wanted to go out and get wet so that my eyes glazed like a seal's and my hair was like a seal's skin. And I wanted something else too but I didn't know what. Something was waiting for me. Just around the corner.

Aunt Nell conjured a small intimate dinner on to the round table in the window. Clear soup, crab salad with lemon dressing, ice-cream meringue. I entertained them with Granny's plots for getting back her teeth. They laughed and we were close-knit and happy.

And all the time, outside in the darkness and the storm, something was waiting. Would I never find it?

CHAPTER SIX

Well, of *course* I thought about Lucas Hawkins.

At one minute past midnight, I rang number five. The rain had settled down to a steady drum beat on my dormer window; I felt safe yet besieged.

He didn't answer for ages. He knew it was me and he thought I was some crummy scheming nurse. I began to get nervous. If he wasn't going to answer, how long dared I let it ring?

Then it clicked and his voice said, 'You again. I thought I'd put a stop to you.'

'You did. But I had to tell someone. I might have found the answer. It's so incredibly corny you'll want to throw up.'

'What are you talking about?'

'Casey and Beamish of course. They're my project. I told you.'

I heard him sigh. Then incredibly, he said, 'I've been thinking about it.'

'You have?' He'd actually put his mind to matchmaking schemes? He'd actually got outside his own body, outside his room?

He said, 'You're tricky. Very tricky. You couldn't care less about this nurse doctor business. Perhaps you *are* this Casey character. And you think I might just be curious enough to come out and size you up.'

I was so mad I nearly choked. Somehow I turned it into a laugh.

'How wrong can you be? Gosh, if I was Casey . . .' Wistfulness cracked my voice. 'Anyway, I'm not Casey. And I'm not Beamish either, before you try any more funnies. And I'm interested in the two of them because it's better than being interested in . . . anything else.'

'Like hell you are,' he said and waited expectantly.

I had to laugh again. 'Yeah. Maybe you're right there. I *am* more interested in me than anyone or anything else.'

'Don't apologize,' he said dryly.

'I'm not apologizing. I *am* interesting. And to prove it I'll tell you how I made a breakthrough with Casey.' I took a breath. 'I made her jealous. How's that?'

'Like you said, so corny I could throw up.'

'So what does it matter if it works? And does it or does it not prove that I am interesting?'

'You needn't be interesting. You could simply have a nice pair of legs.'

'Christ!!'

It was as if a knife came up from under my ribs. The pain was awful and I put down the phone and leaned over it fighting a very real nausea. The rain drummed. I breathed deeply, counting each breath in and out, pushing a little extra out each time to make room in my lungs for a bigger intake. Beneath my nightie the things called legs hung flaccidly, newly washed and powdered, a useless responsibility I had to drag about with me. Because my heart wasn't up to having them amputated and learning to walk on tin ones. I closed my eyes tight shut and tried to remember that they were a mermaid's tail.

The rain drummed. I reached for Dorothy and behind me Zeek guarded my back. I was safe. Safe.

The phone burped discreetly.

I stared at it. He didn't know who I was. He didn't have my number. It must be Bennie wondering whether I was awake and would like tea or coffee. I picked it up gingerly. No one spoke.

'Hello.' I tried to sound utterly sleepy, as if I'd just been wakened from three solid hours of total unconsciousness. But he knew.

'I've tried every damned number. Woken everyone in the blasted hospital. But not you – you weren't asleep. So don't pretend.'

I said furiously, 'It's not a hospital. It's a home. It's our *home*.'

'Why didn't you say you were a patient? Wouldn't it have made things much easier?'

I screamed at him. 'I'm not a patient, Hawkins! You might be a patient, but I am not. I am a resident. Got that?' I waited a bit and thought of something else. 'And I don't want to make things easier for you, boyo. I want to make them harder. Harder! Understand?'

He hadn't heard me. 'You're number seventy-eight. Right at the top. So you manage pretty well. And you think I should too.'

I sobbed, 'I hate you. I hate you because you need not be here at all. Because you've had everything you wanted out of life and now there's something you want more than life and you're sulking because you can't have it!'

He went on reflectively. 'I think you're the screwball I saw when I arrived. Covered in daisies. I thought the place must be a loony bin.'

'Get off this line! I don't want to talk to you ever again – get off this line!'

'All you have to do is to put your phone down.'

I put my phone down. It was surprising it didn't shatter into pieces.

CHAPTER SEVEN

Granny said plaintively, 'It was steak last night. And I couldn't eat it. I mungled one piece around for half an hour and if I hadn't spat it out I'd have missed pudding too.'

'Serves you right.' Mr Pope spoke with great relish. 'If you hadn't given your teeth to this young whipper-snapper –'

'You mean if she hadn't been so careless with them! And I reckon she could get the bleeding things back now if she spoke nicely to Staff Nurse Casey.'

I said, 'You know I won't do that. We're sort of rivals and you don't talk nicely to a rival.'

'Rubbish!' Granny snapped irritably. Hunger obviously made her irritable. Mr Pope cackled unexpectedly and Granny rounded on him and told him just what she thought of people who ninny-picked at their food – fancy hernia or no fancy hernia.

We were sitting in the lounge watching the rain sheet down the terrace windows. Tea was still an hour off and lunch seemed years ago. Rosie and I were supposed to be doing a jigsaw on the coffee table between us, but Rosie had gone to sleep. I wished I had accepted Stella's invitation to swim with the others but I'd been in the pool in the morning and had the curious sensation that my legs were weighted and were going to drag me to the bottom. Also I might have caught a cold yesterday in my thin gear; I was shivery and my chest wasn't expanding properly.

Granny came back to me.

'I know why you won't get my teeth back, Miss Termagant. You think you can needle Casey into taking them to Doctor Beamish and reporting you. You think that will be an excuse for them to get together *and* put you in the limelight. Don't you?' Her chin came at me stabbingly. 'But that puts *me* in the bloody limelight too doesn't it? I get cold-shouldered by the nurses. I'm a naughty old lady who's going senile and must be transferred to some geriatric ward at the earliest opportunity.'

'I'll get them back for you. Stop worrying.' I tried to turn my mind to Casey and Beamish but it was hard. What did Lucas Hawkins look like? Why hadn't he rung me again last night? I tried to forget the long wakeful hours till daylight; the rain on my dormer; Dorothy and Zeek somehow withdrawn from me as I lay with my face turned towards the silent phone. Had he slept? Had he got some kind of peace from needling me as I had needled him?

'It's over a week. I can't help worrying. I was going to tell them I'd dropped the things down the bog –'

Mr Pope yelped, outraged, 'The *what*?'

'Bog. What are you – some kind of nancy-boy that you can't understand plain English when it's spoken to you?'

I said, 'Don't do that. Casey hasn't found out yet who they belong to. She'll know for sure if you announce you've dropped them down the bog.'

'The *bog*?' Mr Pope tried to look horrified through his enjoyment.

'I should tell her you'd taken them. Which is true – almost. When she tells Doc Beamish I shall say you whipped them –'

'She wouldn't tell Beamish. She'd give them back to you and smile at me ever so sweetly –'

'She wouldn't report me?'

'Of course not. Casey is a perfect gentleman.'

Granny's mouth practically turned itself inside out. 'Then why didn't you say so before? That's what I'll do. I'll ask her for them. Now. Where is she?' She started to get out of her chair, pulling frantically at her Zimmer walking aid.

I restrained her. 'You can't do that. It's too tame – you know it is. I'll think of something.'

'It's been over a week. It was funny at first. I admit it. Not any more.' But she subsided into her chair.

'Look. I'll have them for you by –'

'Tonight,' she supplied firmly.

'It's fish tonight. You don't need them for fish. Tomorrow. I'll get them for you tomorrow. How's that?'

'Lunch-time?' Granny nagged.

'Or dinner.' I held up my hand as she half rose. 'Tomorrow. I promise.' I smiled at her engagingly.

Mr Pope said sententiously, 'If you can't stand the heat, keep out of the kitchen.'

Granny gave him a malevolent look. 'I'm going to get even with you, Arthur Pope,' she said.

He looked pleased at the prospect.

I couldn't face tea and went to my room to think. Or rather to face my thoughts which I knew were unpleasant. First and foremost was my stupid handling of Lucas Hawkins; how was it that from being puppeteer I had suddenly become puppet? Why, when I was smarting and burning up from his realization of my incompleteness – when I hated his guts in fact – did I wait for him to ring me again last night? Had I honestly expected an apology, or something equally ingratiating? One thing was certain, I was definitely not going to ring him again. And I was definitely, certainly, one-hundred-per-cent positively, not going to fall in with the Beamish/Parish plan to lure him out of his hole with my marmoset attractions.

The thought of seeing him made me shudder. It would be like Granny Gorman seeing herself in a mirror. He had been allowed to see behind my façade. He knew how very much I hated my incompleteness. How pathetic was my triumph over Casey's spurious 'jealousy'. He knew me.

I closed my eyes and tried to think of a plan to retrieve Granny's teeth and the phone rang. I nearly fell out of my chair reaching for it.

Stella said, 'Mrs Pountney has got a marvellous idea, Fran. Can you come down?'

I felt so flat it was incredible. My watch said five o'clock; another two hours till dinner; I had already spent a fruitless hour thinking and sweating. Could I face another two? But then, could I face Mrs Pountney and Stella – doubtless Penny too – and their dedicated enthusiasm?

'No.'

She hated flat monosyllables, did Stella. She was so used to sifting and analysing every damned thing for her O levels that a mere yes or no left her pantingly dissatisfied. It was my way of punishing her for not being Lucas Hawkins.

'Oh, *Fran*. Don't be mean. We *need* you. You could make it *go*.'

'Make what go?'

'A play. Or an entertainment. Or something. Mrs Pountney says we could put it on for Fête Day. Oh Fran, *please*.'

What could I say? Granny's teeth would have to wait. Also Casey and Beamish. And Lucas Hawkins. I said wearily, 'Give me half an hour. I have to change my pants.'

'All right. But don't be long, Fran, it's nearly time for dinner. I'll be secretary and write everything down, shall I?'

'You do that.' I put the phone down and actually cried at the thought of Stella tortuously taking notes. Then, amazingly, I felt better. I looked round and let my room sink into my consciousness again; the security of it, yet with the rain washing over the dormer like a waterfall, its beleagueredness. There was Dorothy lying comfortably on the bed I'd made all by myself before Casey even arrived this morning; there were the flowers, some of them drooping as if under weight of their own scent; there was Zeek, still smooth and nude inside; there were the wide, shining boards and the low cupboards set under the eaves, and my table laid with scissors and glue and more magazines and . . . everything. It was mine in a way that the wards in previous hospitals could never be. I had left them without regrets; I had left transitory friends without too many regrets also. It was different now. Everything here had meaning and significance that I didn't even understand yet but I knew would be revealed to me bit by bit.

'For instance,' I said quite loudly to hear myself above the rain. 'For instance, that Casey is as soft as butter underneath the enamel.' I began to work off my jeans and pants. 'And for another instance, that Granny Gorman is still May Gorman inside, who could lead the blokes a fair old dance –' I gasped a laugh as I pushed the jumble of clothing from my legs. 'And for yet another instance, that Aunt Nell sat up with Timmy Royston all night long . . .' I hauled clean pants upwards and paused, staring down and seeing nothing. I thought of childless Aunt Nell, her anxious blue eyes, the way she had said to Uncle Roger, 'We cannot ask Fran . . .' Ask Fran what? Ask Fran to help them help someone. And because Fran's pride had taken a fall, she'd decided she wasn't going to consider – think – dream – of helping someone in any way at all.

After a bit I went on dragging the pants up over the objects called knees, rocking from side to side to get them over hips, going through the whole process again with clean jeans; rolling up the cast-offs and putting them in my laundry basket; holding Dorothy against my face as if to hear her voiceless words.

There was no escape. I had met Aunt Nell twice and already knew her goodness. She was irritating and humourless and completely uncool and when it was my turn she would sit with me and hold my hand. And she wouldn't do it to earn herself a place in heaven. She would do it for love.

Angrily I turned my chair away from Zeek and snatched up the telephone and dialled five. As it clicked, I snapped, 'Be in the OT room in ten minutes flat. And don't get any ideas. I'm doing this for Aunt Nell.'

Before I could even make certain it was him on the other end, I slapped down the receiver. How long would my phone last with the sort of treatment it was getting? Then I left for the OT room myself.

They were all there, Mrs Tirrell smiling horsily, Granny toothlessly, Dennis and Rosie gappily. Henry banged on the table for silence.

'We'll put it to the vote now Fran's here. Personally I think a concert would be best. Where we all do our particular thing. A song or a recitation perhaps.'

Stella rose from her notebooks. 'A bit like a competition?' she demurred.

Granny snorted. 'Boring too. You'll have half the audience crying over you.'

'We don't want *that*,' Penny said definitely. 'What ever we do let's make them laugh. Please.'

'I want to be Captain Hook,' Dennis said – and from the groans he'd said it once or twice before. 'And Rosie wants to be Red Riding Hood.'

Penny gnawed at her lip. 'We could be our favourite panto characters perhaps –'

Stella glanced up. 'It'll be individual turns again unless someone writes a linking story.'

'Yes, but we could be the Babes in the Wood,' Penny reminded her, obviously voicing an ancient wish.

Stella smiled. 'Oh yes.'

They both looked at me.

'Listen. I can't write a play and keep the whole place ticking over as well,' I protested. 'Can't we each write our own bit or something?'

'I wanna be Captain Hook. And Rosie wants to be –'

'What can I be?' Granny asked, chin foremost.

'Snow White's stepmother,' I suggested blandly. 'And Mr Pope can be a warlock.'

'There must still be something to link us,' Mrs Tirrell said with gentle persistence. 'It need not be dialogue. Maybe we could sing together – a chorus line –'

'A band!' I looked around at them triumphantly and gave up the idea of Lucas Hawkins arriving. 'We'll have a band! We can all be in it – black and white sheets over us to represent evening dress. Then we throw off the sheets – in turn of course – and emerge as our wishful character.'

Granny's chin wobbled. 'I can play the tambourine. I was in the Salvation Army years ago and I was their star turn.'

'Hey Fran!' Dennis waved his arms above the hubbub. 'I've seen some drums and things in a cupboard in the art room. Let's go and look.'

He bowled himself down the room eagerly. Everyone was laughing and in good spirits. Someone said it was time for dinner and a general exodus began. The rain drummed on the skylights and next door the enormous plastic cover over the swimming pool creaked like ancient ships' timbers in a storm.

Dennis yelled, 'Come *on*, Fran! I can't see in here, it's nearly dark! Where are the lights?'

Granny said to me, 'Don't forget what else you're going to do tomorrow, Miss Termagant.'

Dennis bawled, '*Fran!* It's dark –'

'Oh, for Pete's sake!' I did a three-pointer out of the queue and whizzed down the room and through the swing door with a crash. 'Dennis come on now. We can look for these instruments tomorrow!'

It was dark in the art room. Normally it was lit well with big skylights, but this evening they seemed under water and Dennis, groping with a long cane along the top of the cupboards, looked like a small ghost in his white shirt.

He said, 'They were up here somewhere. I remember when Doreen was dusting she said they should be put away properly.'

From the corner of my eye I saw something.

'She said they were dust-traps. But Mrs Pountney just gave her some polythene bags for them and told her to –'

A faint movement over by the exit doors. Stealthy. Someone was making for the other set of doors that led to the changing rooms and the garden. Someone in a chair.

I said, 'Come on Dennis. Right now. I missed tea and I don't intend to miss dinner. It's fish and chips, which I understand is your favourite.' I kept talking and under cover of my yap, the figure, swathed in a rug I now saw, glided towards the doors.

Dennis put the cane down. 'Oh . . . okay. But don't go that way, Fran. We can go through the swimming pool and –'

'And get very wet crossing the terrace,' I interrupted swiftly. I put on a spurt and opened the swing doors with my step. As Dennis whizzed through I heard the changing room doors close with a sigh.

Dennis said, 'I'd like to go out in the rain. Why can we get wet in the pool but we're not allowed out in the rain?'

I had wanted to go out in the rain at Clevedon. But it didn't stop me worrying about Lucas Hawkins getting soaked to the skin through his rug. I had no doubt that it had been Lucas Hawkins who had sneaked in and listened to our plans for an entertainment. And I had been so tempted to say casually, 'Switch on the lights, would you Hawkins? They're right by your elbow.' But I hadn't. And I didn't know why I hadn't. I hoped very much I hadn't deliberately let him get away with his plan for seeing and not being seen. I mean . . . I didn't want to turn saintly or anything like that.

CHAPTER EIGHT

The next morning I waited till Casey and I were in the bathroom, then I said, 'Have you ever slept with anyone, Casey? A man, I mean?'

'Dozens.' She pulled my nightie over my head, swung my legs into the bath, lowered me after them. She did it so neatly, so expertly. She didn't breathe heavily and neither did I.

'Seriously. Tell me Casey. I need to know – I'm two years older than Juliet and I don't know a thing.'

'You probably know a lot more than I do.' She left me soaping myself while she lined the bath seat with towels and put lanolin and powder to hand. She couldn't have sounded more disinterested if she'd tried.

'Oh, I've read everything. Of course.' I watched her casually. 'But reading is one thing and knowing is another.' She didn't say anything and I had a sudden nasty feeling she might be all buttoned up about it and frigid. That wouldn't do for Beamish at all.

I dunked myself and said briskly, 'Of course I can't ever *know*. Not personally. I realize that. But I thought you could tell me . . . something.'

She hoisted me on to the bath seat and pulled out the plug, then she handed me a towel. She didn't say a word.

I rubbed slowly.

'Casey. Just tell me if it's everything the books say it is. Can't you tell me *that*?'

Her laugh was wonderful, I hadn't heard it before. It would lift Beamish over the moon. She wasn't frigid.

She said, 'Actually, I can't, Fran. Sorry. Why don't you try Bennie? She's got a family and she's had two husbands I believe!'

'She has?' I was almost enticed off course. Not quite. 'But – d'you mean to tell me you've never slept with a man? Honestly?'

'Some girls don't, you know.'

'You're a virgin?'

'You make it sound incredible.' She had me neatly back into the chair, dressing gown strategically positioned. 'I think I should be insulted.'

I flung my arms wide and high. 'Yippee!' I caught her wrist as she pushed the chair back through Zeek. 'Casey, I'm so glad. It makes it just perfect.'

'Makes what perfect?' She turned the chair and eyed me suspiciously. 'I thought I'd got the message over to you, Fran. I won't have you meddling in my affairs! Granny Gorman's teeth are one thing – my personal life is quite another.'

'You know they're Granny's teeth?' I paused in adjusting my bra. 'How long have you known?'

'All the time,' she said briskly. 'Now, d'you want this shirt?'

'No, the sun top. I don't get it. I thought you'd make such a thing of handing them over to her and being smug about it.'

'Then you don't know me quite as well as you imagined, do you?'

She picked up the laundry basket and went to the door.

'Maybe I'm leaving the next move to you. Out of sheer curiosity.'

She began to close Zeek behind her. I called, 'Casey, what do I have to do to get them back? I've already apologized. Do you want me to ask you *nicely* to give them to Granny?'

I caught a glimpse of shrugging shoulders.

'That's one way. Especially if Granny's getting on your nerves with her nagging. I'd like the request to be made in front of her. With a couple of witnesses. Mr Pope and Dennis I think.'

I ground my teeth. Casey was going to make quite sure I never did anything like this again. I knew she was standing out there grinning all over her face thinking she'd won.

'I'm blowed if I will!' I said. After all I had till dinner time. I would think of something.

The door closed very gently. Casey obviously thought she too could afford to wait. I had to laugh. And it might have been my imagination but I thought I heard her laughing too. A marvellous sound. *And* she was a virgin.

Miss Hamlin massaged my buttocks with a ferocity that nearly rolled me off the table.

'Can you feel that?' she gasped, pausing and adjusting the cubicle curtain as Dennis's voice was heard outside.

'Not where you're working. It's flattening my boobs though.'

She ignored me. 'Can you feel this? This? How about this?'

'Yes. Definitely yes. The time before too.'

She repeated several sharp smacks. Drew an invisible line across my rump.

'I think – just think – your sensation area is increasing. Maybe only a centimetre.'

'Is that possible?' I twisted round to look at her. 'You wouldn't kid me, would you?'

'Anything is possible, Fran. Anything.' She looked at me with her solid agate eyes willing me to be convinced.

'But I've had this treatment before. Always. Well, almost always.'

A slight smile. 'Don't worry. I'm not claiming any credit from ten days' work. A cumulative effect . . . I simply don't know. But your record –' She laid her hand on the base of my spine. '– shows *there*. And you can feel here . . . even slightly here . . .'

'Yes. Yes I can – I can.'

'Don't get over optimistic, child. It might mean nothing.'

'Perhaps this is what is waiting for me. Here at Thornton Hall.'

'Waiting for you?'

'Ever since I arrived I've sensed something – I can't explain.'

Her face broke into a smile of pure camaraderie.

'Isn't that the most marvellous feeling? I get it too.'

'You do?' Could Miss Hamlin – pale straw hair and green eyes and professional-woman-status – could she possibly know what I meant?

I expanded. 'The only thing is . . . sometimes – the way I feel – it might be frightening too. Tremendous.'

She didn't try to reassure me; just nodded soberly.

I waited till I was leaving before testing this unexpected kinship.

'Miss Hamlin. You know my special don't you? Staff Nurse Casey?'

She nodded. 'One of our best nurses. A definite gift.'

'And gorgeous looking.'

'Oh yes. She reminds me a little of Marilyn Monroe.'

There was much more to Miss Hamlin than met the eye. I nodded eagerly.

'Tell me something. I mean – give me your opinion. Do you think – er – that is – how about Staff Nurse Casey and Doctor Beamish?'

She looked blank for only a moment, then she pursed her lips and nodded judiciously. 'You could have something there. Both dedicated but she might be able to hold him steady now and then. Yes, that is a possibility.'

I flung aside the curtains triumphantly. Dennis was on the sculling machine, Rosie was with a nurse beneath the lamp.

'Why, if it isn't Captain Hook and Little Red Riding Hood!'

They giggled at me. I felt suddenly all-powerful and certain I was on the right track where Casey was concerned. I turned to Miss Hamlin.

'Thanks. Thanks for everything. And on the strength of your opinion I'm not going to let any grass grow under my feet.'

'Oh dear.'

She was still holding the curtain and watching me when I turned at the door to wave. She looked worried. But that was a compliment too. After all, it showed that she thought I might well get things done.

I paused on the terrace. The garden was breathtaking after the rain. Mr Ottwell was doing something to his tomatoes in the glasshouse. I waved to him but he didn't see me. The unshaded grass on the big lawn steamed gently and the roses dripped dew. I breathed and let it soak into me. I felt good. The cold that had threatened yesterday must have been psychosomatic. I breathed again and my lungs expanded till they touched my ribs. Lovely. Could I feel the tops of my legs or was that all psychosomatic too after Miss Hamlin's words? I dug my knuckles into my hips and moved downward pressing hard. Just where did feeling end? I could not tell, and my heart was still yammering away with the possibility that it could – it might – it *could* happen. Perhaps by the time I was three years older than Juliet when she met Romeo. I would know when I was wetting my pants; and then perhaps I could stop.

I breathed again. I needed air.

I looked down and saw my arms. They were long and beautifully curved and already honey coloured. I stretched them in front of me and looked at the back of my hands; then I brought them slowly to my face, palm to palm, prayerfully. After that they moved by themselves, dancing slowly in the sunlight and with great significance like the hand movements of a Japanese dancer. I watched them with delight. They were leaves, they were butterflies, they were swallows and throbbing larks and spiky starfish. They were frail and then strong, helpless and very capable. They fluttered like snowflakes in the winter and struck swiftly like the rain on the sea.

When they lay in my lap again I saw Mr Ottwell staring. I turned my chair embarrassed, but he shouted and waved his trowel and when I looked up again he put his thumb in the air.

Beamish was writing notes when I got to his door.

'Hullo, Fran. Come on in. I won't be a moment.' His hair was like a Zulu warrior's and his long jaw extended and retracted as he wrote.

I counted ten and could wait no longer. 'It's about

Granny Gorman's teeth,' I blurted and when he raised his head, surprised, I let him have the whole story.

'So you do see, don't you,' I concluded. 'You do see that you'll have to be the one to tell Casey to return the blasted things? Otherwise she's going to make me eat humble pie in front of – *everyone*!'

I raised pleading, rueful eyes to his face, asking for a laugh and surprised to see nothing there.

'Just a minute, Fran.' He came around the desk and sat on the corner next to me, frowning slightly. 'Have I got this right? You took Mrs Gorman's teeth for a joke. Nurse Casey took them from you – knowing to whom they belonged – and has withheld them for over a week?'

'Well, yes. But it wasn't quite like that of course.'

'And during that time Mrs Gorman has been unable to eat any solid food?'

'Oh yes. She had fish. And almost anything she can mangle around with her gums. But –'

'But no raw fruit, no crusts, no roughage at all in fact.' He stood up. 'You did right to tell me this, Fran. Thank you. Leave it with me now.'

'It was only a joke,' I bleated. 'You've got it all wrong.'

'I understand. Though I hope you don't play many jokes of that kind, Fran.' He went ahead of me to the door. 'I'll see Nurse Casey and sort it out. You forget the whole matter. I'll also change your special for you so that there will be no unpleasantness.'

'You'll what?' I felt my temper suddenly explode. 'My God! For an intelligent man who is supposed to have all this blasted *empathy* – you – you're *stupid*!'

I suppose he went on staring as I belted along the corridor and crashed through the swing doors on to the terrace again. I didn't know and I didn't care. When there were women like Granny Gorman and Casey around, it gave me a pain to have to deal with men like Beamish. And Lucas Hawkins.

I tracked Casey down in Sister's office writing in the day book. A hint of a smile appeared in her blue eyes and it hurt like hell to think I had doubtless mucked up the special relationship we had.

She said, 'If you've come to ask me anything – in suitably grovelling phrases – save it a moment while I finish this.'

She was going to turn her winning into a joke. The whole thing had been a game and she had played along so well. Why couldn't Beamish have understood?

I said, 'I can't wait. Because in a moment Beamish will send for you and you'll be on the mat and it's all my fault and I'm sorry.'

The phone rang and she kept level eyes on me while she lifted the receiver and listened and said, 'Very well, Doctor. Right away.' Then she said, 'Save the apologies, Fran. Come on. We're in this together.'

We went along the corridor, past the lounge and dining room, through the door that led to the new block. Casey walked so fast I began to think she was deliberately avoiding my explanation. Beamish's door was closed and she tapped then opened it and held it for me to follow. I left it open as a line of fast retreat.

He said, 'We don't need you, Fran. Thank you.'

My God, he could be chilling.

Casey's voice was colder still. 'I've asked Fran to stay, Doctor.'

He ran his hand through his hair and shrugged. 'It was for your sake, Nurse. However. Obviously Fran has told you what this is all about. For her own perverse reasons she took Mrs Gorman's dentures. The top set. You have seen fit to keep them for over a week which has forced Mrs

Gorman to eat only slops.' He stopped suddenly and a look of bewilderment swept his face. He must have realized for the first time what a ridiculous storm-in-a-teacup this actually was.

Casey said calmly, 'The first part of that statement is true. Frances did take Mrs Gorman's teeth. It was – I understand – a joke in which they both took part. However –' She looked at me and that smile was there again. 'However, the second part is not true. Naturally I removed the teeth from Fran's possession. Naturally I returned them to Mrs Gorman immediately.'

There was a silence. Then I gulped, 'You what? You returned them last week? D'you mean to tell me Casey, you've kept me dangling on a hook all week? You *rotter*!' I snorted a huge laugh and then spluttered, 'And as for that Granny Gorman – the old toad – the snake in the grass –'

Beamish said, 'Wait a minute. Could someone please tell me what this is all about?' He re-combed his hair with spread fingers. 'What it's *really* about?'

Casey looked as if butter wouldn't melt in her mouth.

'Mrs Gorman might not know her teeth are in a beaker in her bathroom with the lower set,' she said demurely. 'But surely if she is so anxious to use false teeth she would have fitted her lower set anyway? I think we can safely assume that Mrs Gorman has been making a fuss about her missing teeth because – like you Fran – she enjoys making a fuss about something.'

That shut me up. And Beamish too. I glanced at him and saw him fitting it all into place. Casey had won. Hands down. Beautifully and without fuss she had scotched Granny, Beamish and me. What a woman. What a wonderful woman.

And then I saw that I had won too. Because here were Casey and Beamish meeting over a pair of false teeth in the most unclinical way possible. Giggles starting burped through my nose.

Beamish's voice trembled slightly. 'I'd like to talk to Nurse Casey about you, Fran,' he said severely. 'If you don't mind.'

'Not at all.' I choked and reversed smartly through the open door. It closed behind me and I waited. Two seconds later Casey started to laugh.

CHAPTER NINE

Seventeen days went by.

My cold wasn't psychosomatic at all. My sense of
well-being disappeared the night of Casey and Beamish,
and the nightmares started. I was in sick-bay in an oxygen
tent and my legs were so heavy I was drowning in my own
tears. People from other hospitals I'd known kept appear-
ing, and the boy who had first seen my likeness to a
marmoset screamed at me, 'Frances Adamson! More like
Fanny Adams! That's what you are – nothing – nothing at
all! Sweet Fanny Adams! Sweet F.A.'

Every now and then they'd go away and there would be
Aunt Nell, blue eyes bulging with anxiety, breasts pendu-
lous as she leaned over me.

'You're a bit better, Frances, dear. Just a bit.'

And I held her hand and wondered if this was it.

I knew Casey and Beamish were around too. My body
recognized Casey's efficient touch; my ears heard Beamish's voice giving instructions and I resigned my physical
self to them gratefully. My mental self surfaced at gradually longer intervals to rest on Aunt Nell. She must have left
me sometimes, but whenever I looked she was there, her
hand reaching for mine, waiting to take on my fear and
petulance and carry it for me.

Once there was someone else with her. Not Uncle
Roger but male and in a wheel-chair. Someone who said

73

above Aunt Nell's distressed croonings, 'Fanny? Sounds Victorian. Distinguished. Like in a Jane Austen novel.' I knew the voice was speaking to me and trying to be encouraging. But it didn't know that above everything else I couldn't bear to be nothing. Not me. Not Frances Adamson.

Aunt Nell's comfort was less bracing and more acceptable.

'Children are always cruel, Frances, dear. Try not to remember things like that.' But still the other voice insisted, 'Fanny. Fanny. It suits her.'

Time passed. One day I knew I was getting better: my back hurt again and I could smell myself and I wanted to cry.

Casey said, 'Mrs Parrish, now that Fran is improving I think you should go back home.'

Aunt Nell's face was ravaged, her sweater sagged at the neck and I could see a mole sprouting hairs.

'Would you like me to stay, Frances, dear?'

I turned my head on the pillow. Had I really clung to her and wept and thought she was my mother still loving me? Had I made a fool of myself?

I said, 'No. Go on home – I don't need anyone.'

'Oh.' She sighed. Relief or regret? I didn't dare catch her eye in case I begged her to stay. She said, 'All right, dear. I'll come back tomorrow.'

I didn't answer her. I wondered whether I could last till tomorrow without her.

Later, Casey did some straightening and propped me up while I drank. I remembered all that business with Beamish. What a fuss about nothing. Was this what had been waiting for me at Thornton Hall? I laughed weakly.

'What's funny, Fran?'

'There's always something waiting for you round the

corner, isn't there?' I whispered. 'Even if it's only pneumonia.'

She settled me gently. 'Another day or two and you'll be back to normal,' she said and turned down her mouth at the prospect. I looked away. No one was going to inveigle me into being involved again.

But then I was back in my room and the campaign started to re-integrate me. Beamish thought a quick dip in the pool would help enormously. He pursed his mouth when I shook my head and said, 'I'll give you another week of this self-imposed solitary confinement, Fran, then I shall carry you down to Miss Hamlin and afterwards take great pleasure in throwing you into the water.'

I couldn't summon a smile.

Stella and Penny came up for a chat. They wondered if they could help me write my part for the play. I couldn't remember what they were on about. Casey brought Granny in a wheel-chair grumbling about anyone making her come all this way when it would be so much easier for anyone to come down to the lounge for a quiet chat. She gave me a list of menus for the past two weeks, then a list of Mr Pope's reactions to them. Frowning and muttering even more fiercely, she left after half an hour.

It was the seventeenth day. In the morning Casey said, 'It's seventeen days since you were ill. Don't you think you could make an effort today Fran and come down to lunch?'

'No thanks.'

'Tea then? Cook has made a gorgeous cake.'

'No, thanks.'

She snapped abrasively, 'Get on with it then. It's known as self-pity.' I didn't rise so she added, 'You want to be alone, is that it? You want your lunch sent up? Tea sent up? Supper sent up? No visitors? Is that what you want?'

I said, 'That's what I want. If you could arrange it.'

She crouched and looked at me hopefully. I let my eyes slide off hers and towards the dormer. She sighed, stood up and left.

I sat there and set myself to thinking of nothing. They say it's not possible. Maybe not, but it is possible to think of a stone. A stone sitting on a lot of land – say, a desert. A dreary grey stone, nothing underneath it, no specially interesting shape. You can use up whole half-hours without having to resort to a book or another thought. I used up the morning and the lunch hour and some time after, and I got quite a kick out of it. Like some people with too much money get a kick out of burning fivers or standing on a bridge and ripping them up and letting them flutter into the water beneath. That's what I was doing with my time. I'd got a limited amount. Why the hell should I try to fill it any more? A pointless exercise. I would waste it.

So there I was, Zeek still unfinished, Dorothy lying on her back with the hole in her tummy indecently exposed, my flowers all gone and my room pristine because I had to have the cleaners.

The phone rang.

'Hullo.'

'Ah. So you're answering at last. Miss Fanny Adams I presume?'

I thought I'd forgotten him. I hadn't. Also I knew suddenly that it had been he who sat by Aunt Nell and heard my ramblings.

'Cheerio,' I said and replaced my receiver. But I was smarting. Otherwise I wouldn't have picked it up when it rang again.

'I want to know why you didn't answer yesterday. And the day before. And the day before that. And –'

'It didn't ring. Maybe I was disconnected to save me taking calls from weirdos.'

'Very wise. Listen, I kept an eye on things while you were out. Casey and Beamish walked in the garden on Wednesday last. From eight p.m. until eight forty-five.'

'Big deal.'

'Well, you started it. The least you can do is take a little interest.'

'I'll let you do that. Good-bye.'

'Fanny – don't go. I want to tell you something –'

'*Don't* call me Fanny! D'you hear me? My name is not Fanny!'

His voice became silky. 'Where's your sense of humour? Besides it suits you. Fanny Adams.'

Tears choked me. 'You think I'm nothing – I know that. You thought Casey and Beamish . . . a lot of fuss about nothing – I know all that –'

He said, 'Shut up. Before you say something you wish you hadn't. I didn't ring to sympathize. Nor, incidentally, to tell you about your matchmaking progress. Something quite different.'

'Oh.' I swallowed my tears.

'Are you going to listen?'

'Don't know.'

'Fair enough. Let's have a go. This concert thing you're doing for Fête Day. No good.'

I remembered; it all came back. The rain on the art room roof. I said, 'So you *did* come to the meeting?'

There was a slight pause. Then he said, 'You know. You knew I was in the art room. Why didn't you say something?'

'You didn't want to be discovered.'

Another pause, longer. He cleared his throat nearly bursting my eardrum.

'Seems I've got a lot to thank you for, Fanny.'

'Don't call me –'

'I'm going to. So get used to it. Thanks, Fanny.'

I exploded with a kind of resignation. 'Oh . . . *bloody hell*!' Because it was no good. I couldn't think of a stone in a desert any more. Life just would not leave me alone.

He was laughing. 'That's better. Now perhaps you'll listen properly. The concert.' I said a rude word about the concert and he went on tranquilly, 'Quite. But you can't give up on it now. And it's just that . . . it'll be so static. A load of wheel-chairs manoeuvring slowly around while Dennis brandishes a sword.'

'What do you suggest?' The sun was shining. I noticed the sun was shining. 'Exactly what do you suggest, genius? I wanted to be Peter Pan and fly but it might be a bit tricky.'

'Perhaps. So where is the place you can all move without chairs? Fast and easily?' My mind was a complete blank and he said exasperatedly, 'Come on Fanny! The pool! Water! You all swim and the light in there is interesting. You've got the changing rooms right behind – quite enough space at the end and sides for seating – you can have loads of comedy pushing each other in –'

'How do you know we can all swim? Have you been spying there too?'

'I've *watched* a couple of times –'

'I call it spying. And you spied on me when I was in sick bay.'

'I don't want to be seen. I mustn't be seen. You *know* that.'

'The nurses see you. Aunt Nell.'

'They're different. It's their job.'

'It's not Aunt Nell's job.'

'She was wrapped up in you. I don't think she *saw* me.'

I breathed twice. 'Anyway . . . you had to risk that if you wanted to see me,' I said slowly.

78

He didn't speak for ages. At last in an offhand voice he said, 'I thought you might die or something stupid.'

My heart beat hard under my nightie. It was three o'clock in the afternoon. What the hell was I doing in my nightie?

I said very quietly, 'Hawkins. You're a nit. You don't have to spy on *us*. We're all handicapped. Granny can walk with her Zimmer but she's buckling up with arthritis.'

His voice was quiet too; subdued and cracking. 'Oh God, Fanny. I'll never get used to it.'

I could have melted with pity. I said hardily, 'You've had time. A month. And before you came to Thornton Hall. I've had pneumonia for seventeen days and they're nagging me to get out again. And you've had a month.' I counted three and said sensibly, 'Now. When is the next meeting about the concert? Come to that. Tell them about your idea. It'll break the ice –'

'No!' It was a shout. He calmed down audibly. 'Listen. Try to understand. Supposing . . .' his voice quietened right down and I pressed the receiver hard against my ear. 'Supposing you had an accident. Lost your hands.'

'My *hands*?'

'Your hands. They're lovely. They talk for you. You use them all the time without knowing it. Supposing you lost them.'

I was absolutely silent, trying not to imagine it.

'You see, Fanny? That's how it is for me. I played football and tennis. Swam –'

'You could still swim,' I said quickly.

'What? You must be joking. I'd up-end like a bleeding duck and plummet to the bottom. Charming.'

'Oh, *Hawkins* –'

'Call me Luke.'

'It's a nancy-name. Hawkins, don't you realize that it's

79

in the water you learn to balance. You've *got* to come in the pool. You've *got* to stop being ashamed. Okay, I'd hate to lose my hands, not only because I'd have to do things like Stella does – and Penny – but because I'm vain about them. Is that why you won't show yourself? Is it vanity?'

'Look. Sod that, Fanny. Don't start trying to needle me into the open. It'll be the end of our beautiful friendship if you do.'

'Beautiful friendship? Is this what you call a beautiful friendship?' I hoped to turn the subject; because naturally I intended to needle him into the open. He wasn't fooled.

'I *mean* it. If you don't leave me strictly alone, I'll never phone you again.'

'And I couldn't stand that,' I said with heavy sarcasm.

'No, I know. You've spent a lot of time waiting for your phone to ring. I wouldn't like to think you had to do that again.'

My eyes stretched wide. 'What d'you mean? I was the one who rang you. Remember?'

'Not always though. Not the night of the storm for instance.'

'How did you know –' I cut my words off short, remembering that ghastly night I had waited for the phone to burp.

'I wasn't sure. You just confirmed it.'

'You are a rat, Hawkins,' I told him levelly. 'You are a sadistic rat.'

'Listen, Fanny Adams, you'd kept me waiting before then. I was getting so I couldn't take my eyes off the phone.'

'Good-bye, rat.'

'Good-bye, Fanny. And it *is* a beautiful friendship, so don't wreck it.'

The line went dead. I replaced my receiver and stared at

it for a long time. Casey came in to see what I'd like for tea. I said, 'I'll get dressed and come downstairs. Then I can make up my mind about the cake.'

She checked herself on a double-take and said dourly, 'I knew it wouldn't be much longer.'

I was busy with my pants. 'Count your blessings, Casey. You've had seventeen days. If you haven't got very far in that time, you *need* me.'

She knelt and held out my jeans. 'The place is dull without you. I'll admit that.'

Her face was like a flower framed in golden hair and white cap. I grinned at it. 'I love you, Casey.'

She tightened her full mouth and flipped the jeans expertly up my legs. Maybe she thought I was going soft.

I said insidiously, 'Did you enjoy your walk with Doctor Beamish? I do hope no one saw you. You know how quickly rumours spread in a place like this.'

She stood up abruptly and grabbed my nightie. I decided to go no further. But whole new prospects were opening out. And the biggest one of all was Lucas Hawkins. And how to force him out of his shell.

CHAPTER TEN

It was hard work selling them Hawkins's idea for an aqua show. Mrs Tirrell did not think I should swim. I told her Beamish had said it would be good for my breathing.

'Rubbish,' Granny commented. 'Hot poultices on your chest. That's what you need my girl. If I had you in my care you'd be out and about in three weeks.'

'I am out and about, Gran. And it's less than three weeks since I got ill.'

'Everyone's swimming mad these days,' Granny went on, dropping two stitches from her left knitting needle. 'Too much water isn't good for a body.'

Mrs Tirrell explained *sotto voce*, 'Mrs Gorman doesn't swim so she's probably feeling left out.'

'*You* don't have to get wet,' I told Granny kindly. 'You can be the one who pushes us in. Just tip up our chairs and –'

'I have no intention of getting wet, Miss Termagant!' snapped Granny. 'And as for tipping up chairs – with my arthritis –'

'You'll manage all right with Mr Pope.'

'Arthur Pope? You'll never get him into this!'

'I've already seen him. And he agreed.'

I didn't mention that he'd agreed only when I informed him that Granny had asked for his help.

'He did?' She sucked in her mouth consideringly. 'Oh, well . . .'

I continued to rub at my triangle with Silvo, well satisfied. I had intended to broach the subject with small groups and it had worked. The kids were no problem, but the older ones seemed to think it was their duty to object to everything for the first five minutes. Mr Pope had been a pushover; he must really fancy Gran. Henry was doubtful. Mrs Tirrell and Granny began to talk themselves into it. Mrs Pountney was holding back on a decision until she saw what the 'ducking' entailed.

I rang Hawkins during the rest period after lunch.

'Everything's settled,' I said, jumping the gun. 'Mrs Tirrell wants to be the old woman who lived in a shoe. Henry – Robin Hood. Penny and Stella – Babes in the Wood.'

'Hang on. I'm not with it.'

'Are you okay? Shall I ring later?'

'Hey. Consideration from Fanny Adams? I must sound like death itself.' He was reviving.

I said, 'Yes, you do. And we don't want a rotten script do we?'

'Listen. I've never written a script in my life –'

'Have you got anything else pressing at the moment? No? Then it looks like now is the time to start writing scripts. Got a pen?'

'Look. Fanny. I gave you the lousy idea. Can't you do anything for yourself?'

'I can organize people. And I'm organizing like mad. So write down . . . Frances Adamson – Peter Pan.'

'What?' He sounded outraged. 'I only thought of the bloody aqua idea so that you could be the Lorelei!'

I'd opened my mouth to reply before he finished. Now I closed it again. Then I took a long breath.

'How did you know about the Lorelei? Casey . . . Casey told you. You've been spying in more ways than one, Hawkins. I don't like it.'

There was a grin in his voice. 'I know. It's pretty low isn't it? Something you'd never stoop to. And I'll tell you something, Fanny. I didn't have to ask her. She told me.'

'Casey wouldn't. She's not like that.'

'I got that impression. About most things. But not when it comes to you. I know things about you, you don't know yourself.'

'Oh . . .' I was going to come out with some expletive that would make him laugh properly, but I didn't. I suddenly realized why Casey was acting so uncharacter-istically. Beamish had roped her into the plan for getting Hawkins out into the open. Socializing him. Integrating him. Call it what you like. But I didn't like. Not now. Strange that – I'd been tickled pink at first, then cringing because he'd seen through me, and now . . . now I wanted him to come out all right. But not for them. For me.

He said, 'Fanny? You still there?'

'Yeah. I'm here. I don't like it, Hawkins.'

'What? Casey doing to you what you did to her?' He snorted a laugh. 'Surely you can see why? If I get interested enough in the crazy girl in seventy-eight who fills her room with flowers and whips old lady's dentures, I'm going to want to meet her. I'm going to come out of my room and into the lounge. Where I can be Got At.'

'Oh, well. If you see through it. I suppose it's okay.'

His clear summing-up brought it into perspective. It was still private, still our joke.

I said, 'You wouldn't let yourself be fooled by such an obvious ploy, huh?'

'You told me you were interesting long before Casey mentioned it. Besides, I've seen for myself. Four times.'

The conversation was now fascinating. 'Tell me exactly when and where. The art room of course. And when I was ill. What about the other twice?'

'I can't remember,' he said airily. 'It's not important is it?'

I ground my teeth. 'Not at all. Uh . . . but you saw what I meant then?'

'Meant?'

'You know. About being interesting.'

'I can't honestly recall my exact impressions at the time.'

I could hear him laughing silently. I said, 'I hate you, Hawkins. You do *know* that? You're quite *clear* about that?'

'Sure,' he said equably. 'Now. Skirmish over. I'll write a script so long as you don't quibble. About anything.'

'Umm. Well. Okay. Up to a point. Nothing topless.'

'Mermaids are always topless Fanny. I realize you're an ignoramus but surely you know that?'

'I'm not an ignoramus. Just because I don't go to school doesn't mean I'm ignorant. I know more than most people.'

'Tell me about Nietzsche.'

'Oh, for Pete's sake –'

'Thomas Aquinas?'

'Look here, Hawkins –'

'Dylan Thomas? The Romantic poets? *Othello? The Wife of Bath?*'

'Yes! Yes – I know about them! I do! I love "The Green Fuse" and I hate Iago and *The Wife of Bath* is just my cup of tea. So there.'

I heard him sigh. 'One sentence. One little sentence plus a colloquialism dismisses a range of great English writers –'

'Oh, shut up. If you want a thesis, come back in a year's time.'

85

'Okay. Will do. Start now. Limit yourself to one of them – Dylan Thomas, I'd guess. Read everything he ever wrote. A couple of biographies – reviews, obituaries, everything like that. But get started.'

I said slowly, 'Beamish has been talking to you too. About my education. My God.'

He said briskly, 'I haven't got time to talk to you now. There's a play to write before bed time. Good-bye.'

He got his phone down a split second before I did. On the whole I was the loser of that encounter. Though on the other hand he *was* going to write a script.

Granny was a surprisingly unwilling recipient of my steak at dinner that night.

'You've got a lot of ground to make up, Miss Termagant. Come along now – cut it up small and try.'

'I can't eat it. Honestly Gran. I'll have your ice-cream if you like.'

'I'd forgotten how you two swop your meals,' Mr Pope commented. 'It's disgusting.'

'There's no pleasure when she's giving it away,' Granny grumbled. 'It's just my luck to sit at a table with a pair of ninny-pickers like you two.'

Mr Pope said, 'I notice you don't move elsewhere.'

'Neither do you,' Granny came back belligerently. She turned to me. 'For three weeks he's been carrying on about the way I enjoy my food. And he's still here. Still grumbling.'

'Hark who's talking,' Mr Pope remarked bitterly. 'She never stops. If I eat something, then I'm not doing myself any good. If I don't . . .'

'Ninny-picker.' Granny was reduced to name calling as she got to grips with the steak. 'Moaning minnie.'

I raised my brows at Mr Pope. 'I told you she fancied you. I can see I'm playing gooseberry. Excuse me.'

Granny tried to catch my arm and bleated, 'Fran, you haven't had the ice-cream.'

But I grinned over my shoulder. Bennie would be up at ten with coffee and custard creams and there were two hours of daylight before then. I wanted to pick the flowers as they closed for the night and sit on the horseshoe lawn and make a daisy chain. And more than that: I wanted to watch my hands dance in the evening sunlight. And be thankful for them.

CHAPTER ELEVEN

I couldn't wait to see if he'd ring me. Pride or no pride I
dialled number five soon after eleven when I knew Bennie
would have gone to the staff room for a couple of hours.
He was surprised and still weary. Much wearier than he'd
sounded that afternoon. Of course he'd been working on
the script all afternoon.

I said, 'I've been out in the garden this evening. First
time for ages. It was marvellous. Lots of changes. There
are red hot pokers in the lavender hedge. And a new crop
of pansies. Brown with yellow blotches. Like butterflies.'

He said, 'Hey, you're really better. I'm glad. Fanny, I've
got to ring off. If I don't sleep I'll go mad.'

'Have they given you sleeping pills?'

'Yes. They're here. I didn't want to take them till I'd
phoned you. And that's supposed to be at midnight.'

'Rules are for breaking. Listen, Hawkins, don't take the
pills. You won't need them if you get outside and breathe
this air. Honestly. I guarantee you a full night's sleep if you
follow these directions absolutely.'

'Don't be a fool. The place is locked up. The dogs would
let fly.'

'That's really funny. My second night here I did a
midnight ramble and didn't see them. That was when I
found out the number of your room. Also that they keep

the french door in the lounge on the latch. The lounge is opposite the staircase.'

'Fanny . . . I can't.'

'It's not fair, Hawkins. You've seen me and I haven't seen you.'

'My stumps are aching to glory.'

'Don't give me that. You know you need fresh air. You're scared. That's your trouble. You're scared.'

'Dammit all, what do you want from me, girl? I've gone along with these crazy phone calls. I've spent the whole afternoon and half the night getting something down on paper for your lousy concert –'

'I'm leaving right now, Hawkins. I'll wait for you on the horseshoe lawn. Where you saw me when you arrived. If you don't come – don't bother to phone excuses.'

I put the receiver down. The moths beat feebly against the dome of my dormer trying to reach the light. I stared at them knowing how they felt. Whether Hawkins came or not made no difference. There was no future for people like me.

I left the window wide for him. My wheels made no sound on the flagged terrace and I coasted down the ramp and straight over the gravel path on to the grass. The small crunch as I crossed the loose stones was minimal. I was almost certain the open ground floor windows along this side of the house belonged to Granny, Mr Pope and the other adults.

There was no moon as yet but the night was light with stars. Anyone taller than the lavender and box hedges would be completely visible, so that made me all right. There must have been quite a bit of rain while I'd been ill because my wheels had to be shoved every inch over the turf, but I didn't mind. The air was sharply chill and I needed to keep warm. Belatedly I wondered whether it would be good for Hawkins out here after so long in-doors.

I waited.

There were a lot of sounds. The aspen trembled to every breath of wind and made it seem colder than it really was; somewhere towards the Avon a fox barked, and nearer – much nearer – a pair of hedgehogs snuffled out their courtship. I wondered, if they bit ankles, whether I should know about it. Once when I was about four years old, a kitten slithered off my lap and left claw marks on my leg which turned septic because no one knew about them. There was an awful fuss. The nurses seemed to think it was my fault. I smiled deliberately into the darkness and listened to the traffic on the motorway. He wasn't going to come.

And then, somewhere behind Mr Ottwell's massed flowers, gravel crunched beneath a set of wheels.

I was so relieved I slumped in my chair, lowering my head and closing my eyes while my nerves trembled into quiescence. It had seemed like an hour waiting there. And with each minute that passed I felt I'd burned my own boats. If Hawkins had not come he must have accepted my ultimatum. That would be . . . that.

When I raised my head he was just getting on to the big lawn. I heard him grunt as his wheel stuck in the dewy turf and I remembered that his arms would not be as compara-tively strong as mine, also that his stumps were aching to glory. I pushed myself forward furiously to meet him.

His face was a white blur against the darkness of the hedge. I got the impression of fair hair curling down quite a long, a big head, a cricketer's head rather than a foot-baller's, bony, hunched shoulders, very long arms.

He gasped, 'Christ, everyone will see you! What the hell are we doing *here*!'

Of course he'd observed me before and had no need for the questing, curious pause.

I said, 'Because we both knew it. Never mind now. Turn back on to the path and we'll go down the laurel walk.' That meant I wouldn't be able to examine him much, it was very dark between the thick laurel. But I had already seen why he couldn't accept himself any more. The rug which had swathed him securely in the art room that night, had been replaced by a thinner honeycomb blanket which made a plateau of his lap and then tucked under his stumps. He was a torso with a head and arms. As he struggled ahead of me to mount the slight camber of the path I looked at the dark outline of the remaining third of him. He had been tall and strong and the world had been at his feet. And now he had no feet.

I said, 'Hawkins . . . thanks for coming.'

He didn't speak as he slewed his chair to face down the path. Then I felt him turn towards me, and for a long moment we faced each other, black silhouettes in the sooty shadow of the laurel. The sharp smell of the pungent leaves almost over-rode his disinfectant and bandage aura.

I whispered timidly. 'It *will* make you sleep. For one thing the smell is so marvellous.'

Another silence and I was terrified he was gritting his teeth against pain, just waiting for strength to get back to the house.

Then he hissed, 'Don't you dare go soft on me, Fanny Adams!'

'There's no need to be insulting!' I came back, quick as a flash, my heart lifting again to the excitement of the night and the strange sounds and the wonderful freedom. 'I just don't want you backing down now. This is only a preliminary. What I really want to do is to get outside in a thunderstorm.'

'Oh, God,' he said, grimly resigned.

I went ahead of him and bent to the business of moving. I knew at the end of the laurel walk there was a path around the edge of the reedy lake I could see from my dormer, and the water would reflect the starlight. I wanted to see him.

He wasn't far behind – his arms were stronger than I'd thought – and I deliberately kept my back to him until we were on the edge of the water. Then I did one of my on-the-spot turns.

He just missed me. 'Clever,' he panted. 'Very clever. What would have happened if I'd gone in the water?'

'I'd have pulled you out of course. Have you brought the script?'

That gave him something to do while I looked at him. He started fishing about inside his sweater, muttering something about bossy females. I looked at him.

There were signs of neglect. He had held out against a hair-cut but someone – not Casey – had shaved him and nicked his chin and neck in several places. Unless he was spotty. He was thin too; his bones stuck out at his wrists and his shoulders were sharp beneath his sweater; his fingers looked skeletal. He had a full mouth, relaxed and sullen now as he searched for the separate pieces of paper. His brows were heavy and shadowed his eyes, giving a further impression of withdrawal. Then his head came up and I saw his eyes were blue.

'What are you staring at?' he said tightly, immediately angry.

'You.'

He stared back. Then with a gesture of surrender he handed the script to me.

'Listen, Fanny. I can't keep this up. Sorry.' He half turned back towards the path.

'Wait. I haven't finished. I'm only half way down.'

'That's all there is!' His voice was bitter-aloe. 'They end *there*! Okay?' He shoved the blanket closer around his stumps, then winced.

I said quickly, 'You can't shock me, I swim with Penny and Stella. I want to look at you. Not your accident.'

He tried for a laugh. His teeth showed in a grimace. They were good teeth, even and white. A long nose and jutting chin.

He said, 'Oh, *Fanny* . . .' His neck was strong and full of funny knotty cords. He was too pale. Even in this light I could see that. He'd been indoors for three weeks, but I still had some tan from that hot June. He repeated, more loudly, 'Fanny. I cannot sit here while you stare. I can't do it. I'll have to go.'

'It's okay, I've finished. And you'd better hurry up and get outside pretty soon, else you're going to look like a slug.'

'A slug?'

'One of those white ones that get under stones. Nasty.'

'Thanks. Thanks a lot.'

I put the script carefully into my tidy bag. Then I aligned my chair with his, sat up straight and assumed the voice of a tour guide.

'Over there we have the Avon bridge carrying the M5 motorway into Somerset and Devon. Before that it stops at Clevedon, where live the Parrishes in a nice house overlooking the sea. You should go there.'

'What! And have Aunt Nell fussing me worse than my own mother?'

'You'll have to train your mother like I'm training Aunt Nell.'

'Train my mother?'

'Not to feel guilty.'

93

He paused, thinking about this and did not argue about it. But his voice was leaden with sarcasm when he spoke again.

'And how do you go about that?'

'Well . . . you're cheerful. You beat them at table tennis and billiards. You learn to use your chair like a bumper car –'

'Good God. Little Lord Fauntleroy. I never thought it of you, Fanny.'

I was suddenly tired to death. It was like pushing a stone up a hillside. I took a very deep breath and went in at the deep end.

'Stop being a defeatist. When are you going to get up? Go to physio and have a go on the parallel bars? Try some crutches? Get fitted for your tin legs?'

He sighed. 'Now we come to it. The object of the exercise. The pep talk. Christ, Fanny. I thought you might be a little less obvious.'

'I want to know. So I asked . . . Are you going to tell me?'

'No. Because you already knew. You're probably the one person who has no need to ask such stupid questions.'

'Sorry, Hawkins. I've obviously missed out somewhere. I don't know the answer. Naturally I am assuming that having walked, you would like to walk again. I'm not in a position to judge of course, never having walked at all.'

He breathed audibly. 'You bitch,' he said.

I turned my chair without haste and began to move away.

'Time we were going in. Take deep breaths and think quiet thoughts.'

He tried to catch me up. 'Look here, Fanny . . . I'm sorry. But you know bloody well you're being unfair.'

I kept going slowly along the tunnel of laurel. The smell was overpowering. I said softly, 'When, Hawkins? When are you going to start learning to walk again?'

He couldn't pass me. He could have stopped but maybe he felt like I did, that once he stopped he'd never start again.

'Go to hell,' he suggested tersely.

I shut up until we were on the terrace. The window was still open, no one was about. We'd done it. We were back and undetected. I stopped and looked round at him. We were both having difficulty with our respiration. He stared back and suddenly the moon came up from behind the house and illuminated his face. It was beautiful. He looked at me with his blue eyes and smiled unwillingly.

'We made it. Without anyone knowing.'

'That's just a taste of freedom, Hawkins.' I was missing the phone. I wanted to say something and make a quick getaway. I manoeuvred my chair into position for a straight run through the window and across the lounge. He would have to stop and close up. I'd be up the ramp and in the lift before he knew it. I controlled my breathing with an effort of will. 'Just a taste of freedom. Think how it will be when you can get out of that chair and walk again.'

He threw himself back in exasperation. 'Fanny, stop it. Please. You know I don't want to stump around, always in pain, half a mile behind anyone else –'

'But you've *got* to, Hawkins! You *must* walk again!'

'Why? Can you give me one good reason why I should put myself through all that?'

'Of course I can.' I put my hands on my wheels and got ready. 'How the hell can you carry me over the threshold if you can't walk?'

I pushed hard and shot through on to the oak boards of the lounge. There was complete silence except for the soft brush of my wheels. I was out in the corridor taking a run at the ramp when I thought I heard something. I backed into the lift, put my hand on the button to close the doors and then paused. But there was nothing. No laughter. No whispered recall. My outrageous remark lay somewhere on the terrace. Ridiculous. Foolish. And, quite rightly, discarded.

CHAPTER TWELVE

He didn't phone that night. Nor the next. On the front of
the script he'd written, 'Keep me out of this Fanny – I'm
giving it to you – it's yours.' I couldn't phone him to argue
about it, so that's how it had to be. Everyone thought it
was marvellous and thought I was marvellous. If only I
hadn't made that stupid remark on the terrace, I'd have had
him right out in the open directing the blasted play. But he
didn't ring, so how could I?

Aunt Nell donned a ghastly swimming costume and
joined us at the pool with Uncle Roger. She showed him
what I – what Hawkins – proposed for the ducking
ceremonies.

'Mrs Pountney is worried – I'm not really surprised.'
She trod water anxiously and ran her hand along the edge.
'Mrs Gorman and Mr Pope are not up to judging the
correct positioning of the chairs.'

Uncle Roger stared at Hawkins's plan and hummed and
haa'd and said it was out of the question. Impossible. I
began to bleat protests because I wasn't about to have
Hawkins's script altered by an inch. Aunt Nell smiled at
me and touched her finger to her lips. So then Uncle Roger
knelt on the bank and laid his arm along the concrete.

'Listen, Fran, how about this. A rubber buffer just here –
say about eight feet long. And there – and nowhere else – is
your ducking entry. If I can find some way of anchoring

it – it will have to be very strong of course – Granny and old Pope can run the chair up right against the buffer and the occupant will shoot out. You can disguise the buffer as rocks or hedge or whatever.'

'Hey. That's great!'

Aunt Nell smiled and spluttered. 'Uncle Roger is an engineer, you know, Fran. He has his own factory. When he gets an idea –'

'I'll have to ask permission to chop up the concrete a bit,' he mused. 'But if I promise to put it back as I found it, that shouldn't be too difficult. How long have I got, Fran?'

'Till next Saturday.'

He made an appalled face but he'd known he had only five days anyway. He simply wanted Aunt Nell and me to be full of admiration for his energy and efficiency and enterprise. We were.

Again that night I waited until one-thirty before switching off my light. I knew by five past midnight that it was hopeless but I waited anyway. Zeek had flowers inside as well as out now, and he guarded the doorway impassively. The moths beat on my dormer. Dorothy sprawled, the wound in her stomach showing all too clearly through my botched stitches. I tried to tell myself it was all the same, gloriously isolated and secure. But it was more than that now. It was also lonely. And a small wind blew through me though the room was draught proof.

Saturday came at last. The weather was just right; sunny with a bit of a breeze to cool down flushed faces and a few very high white clouds holding no rain. The visitors started arriving at two o'clock, and at half-past two the Fête was opened by an actor from the Bristol Old Vic. We showed them around meticulously. Our rooms, the library, the lounge and dining room and games room; the chapel which was a copy of a church in Istanbul. The OT rooms were laid out with work. The room where the kids had their school was choc-a-bloc with marvellous displays . . . everything. There were cream teas on the terrace and the band from the local Boys' Brigade played raucously and marched on the lawn. There were stalls and a tombola and raffles and pinning the tail on the donkey. We tried to be everywhere at once, sample everything, and as we passed each other we communicated our mutual excitement. We'd been in the pool area all morning, maddening the helpers by trying to fix it up ourselves.

Aunt Nell had made me a lovely fish-tail. I'd practised in it a couple of times and it gave no extra resistance to the water and kept my legs together so that swimming was easier than usual. It was made of that glittery lycra stuff and when I pulled myself up on the raft the water ran off it in glistening drops. Casey helped me to pull it on and fasten it around my waist under the fringe of green raffia seaweed which draped my shoulders. I hadn't had my hair cut since before I came to Thornton Hall and it was below the nape of my neck but not long enough to do much draping. I'd vetoed the wig. The raffia had been Mrs Tirrell's compromise.

She looked marvellous in a dress with an enormous skirt full of pockets, each one containing a doll which she would produce and throw into the water as she wailed, 'I don't know what to do . . . o . . . o.' Dennis was in tights and a black jacket and cocked hat with a plastic sword by his side. Rosie of course had a red hooded cape which she could discard easily in the water. Penny and Stella wore identical smocks made of cheese cloth and ridiculous little hats with enormous bows, and Henry had a stuffed parrot on his shoulder as Long John Silver. Gran and Mr Pope hardly needed to dress up as 'Malice' and 'Mischief'.

Everyone came in and found seats while we sat there draped in our black and white sheets and percussioned away to a record of *The Blue Danube*. We were nervous but everyone smiled and some waved and Granny brandished her tambourine and showed her gums and we relaxed. I spotted people I knew. Beamish was in the front grinning proudly. Miss Hamlin stood at the side tapping her foot to the music. But no Aunt Nell, no Uncle Roger. There were three empty seats right at the back next to the door. The roof was about to blow off with rhythm and excitement. And then they came; Uncle Roger first holding the door back with one outstretched arm; then Aunt Nell hovering nervously. And then . . . then . . . someone else. Someone on crutches, one trouser leg pinned, a single artificial leg stumping, pushing, heaving, until the body could lurch forward on to the crutches again. Forward, struggle, upright . . . forward, struggle, upright. Three whole steps and then he waited and looked for me.

I could see his face clearly now. It wasn't so white, and I fancied it wasn't so thin. His hair was golden blond and very curly. His shoulders were squarer than ever because of the up-thrusting crutches. He was wearing grey flannels and a white shirt and a tweedy jacket. I knew he was saying to me silently across the beat of sound, 'This is what I've been doing for the past two weeks. This is why I didn't ring you. I wanted to show you instead.'

How could the show be a flop after that? It had to be a success with our writer sitting there watching his creation come to life. By the time the actual acting began, the audience was with us every inch of the way. Stella and Penny opened, because they could bolster each other up. They had expanded a ditty which started, 'Two little maids from school are we, Sitting forlornly beneath this tree.' They erected a coverless umbrella hung with paper leaves amid a roar of appreciation. 'No cake, not even a cup of tea; No hope of rescue for her . . . or me . . .' They went on, large-eyed, their poor hands hidden beneath the masking sheets. By the time they flung off their covering and ducked their heads to pull on their hats, no one noticed they were armless. Surely Hawkins realized that?

Granny came to the edge of the pool and bawled confidentially, 'They'll never be the Babes in the Wood. But I can be Malice. And *he* can be Mischief.' And she and Pope took a handle each, drew back the wheel-chairs and shoved hard against our rubber buffer. Penny and Stella took off beautifully, curled themselves into balls and plopped into the water amidst gasps of shock, then thunderous applause. They came up and paddled around the perimeter like little ducks, trailing their cheese cloth plumage behind them. Miraculously their hats stayed in place. They were soon joined by Dennis, brandishing his sword and slicing magnificently at the water; Rosie, more gently lowered in by some of the helpers to bob like an autumn leaf, her head pillowed on a foam float; Mrs Tirrell swimming after her dolls, and Henry making awful parrot noises.

The idea was that I should bring peace from confusion which was a bit of an anticlimax with the audience clapping and stamping all the time and the atmosphere in the pool riotously enjoyable. But I wasn't playing for them, I was playing to Hawkins alone. As soon as I surfaced, Bennie turned up the volume on *The Blue Danube* and my hands went with the familiar melody all by themselves. I lay on my back and let them move as they would, and gradually everything quietened and went very still so that my fingers and wrists and arms were the only moving objects. As if drawn by them, I shoulder-swam to the float, stopping to pull myself up and arrange my tail, then continuing again. The others began to glide towards me.

We ended with a tableau; Malice and Mischief cowering in their chairs behind us.

The applause was deafening and went on and on until we didn't know what to do with ourselves. At last Beamish stood up and lifted his hands. 'Ladies and gentlemen . . .' he made a little speech telling them about our rehearsals and thanking 'our good friends the Parrishes' for their help. Then he said we would be swimming for a while and if anyone wished, they could stay behind, but he would remind them that our evening meal was served at . . . I kept my eyes on Hawkins. When he stood up with help from Uncle Roger one side and Aunt Nell the other – how he must *hate* that – I wanted to applaud *him*. It wasn't fair that no one had recognized his part in the proceedings. They weren't even noticing what he was doing right at this minute. He didn't look at me again. As he started the rhythmic swing, push, stand . . . swing, push, stand, all over again, Aunt Nell turned and waved and then blew a kiss. I blew her one back.

He rang at eleven-thirty.

'How about a turn around the garden before bed?' he asked casually.

'Um . . . well . . . All right. I suppose my knitting can wait till morning.'

'Oh, I should think so,' he said.

He was already by the window in the lounge and held it open for me. He was in his chair. We didn't say much and when we did we didn't fence any more. I remember there was a bird singing. 'Nightingales,' he identified. 'They like this weather. And the avenue.' I realized the faint breeze of the afternoon had gone and the stillness no longer had a waiting about it. It was peace.

'You know about birds?' I asked.

He didn't make a crack, just said, 'A little. It's something I can follow up now.'

I remember the heady scent of the stocks. And telling him what each flower-bed contained in the inky darkness of the sheltering hedges.

'Some of the staff call you the flower girl,' he said with a smile in his voice.

'I'm very interested in flowers. Maybe next year I'll try for a Botany O level.' I knew I wouldn't but it was a small offering in exchange for his enormous effort.

I remember the myriad small sounds by the marshy lake and the way the water carried the noise of the motorway traffic as it pounded down to the West for holidays, or pounded back.

We returned slowly between the acrid laurels.

'The Parrishes say their car will take two wheel-chairs,' he mentioned hesitantly. 'Could we visit them together?'

'Yes.' A small spurt of excitement pierced the peace of my soul. 'If only it would rain again. We might persuade them to take us out in it.'

He didn't laugh. 'Not likely. You might get pneumonia again.'

'Me? Don't be daft. That was a left-over from hospital. After two months at Thornton Hall I'm as strong as an ox.'

Why did I say that? To boast? To mislead him?

He didn't argue, just ran his chair up the ramp and along the terrace. I waited for him in the lounge to close the window and we exchanged silent smiles in the white moonlight. Then he went along the corridor to room five. And I took the lift to room seventy-eight.

CHAPTER THIRTEEN

Granny surveyed us both with chin unusually well tucked in.

'What do you mean, it's a pity it didn't rain? You've had a day by the seaside, got yourselves nice and brown and you wanted it to rain? Didn't you enjoy it?'

Mr Pope muttered as a sort of background to this, 'Ungrateful, that's what the young people are today. Ungrateful.'

Hawkins said solemnly, 'I quite agree, Mr Pope. One wonders what will happen to the world if such ingratitude continues to –'

'I *told* you, Granny! We can usually persuade Aunt Nell to agree to things and it's our only chance –'

Dennis pushed his chair backwards and forwards coming nearer to Mr Pope's toes each time. 'They want to go out in the rain,' he explained impatiently. 'Well, Fran does. And I do too. I want to drink the rain.'

'Unhygienic,' Hawkins mentioned. 'Probably unhealthy too.'

'Mad,' chipped in Mr Pope.

'I don't understand it.' Granny hated having to agree with Pope.

'Reveals an unexpectedly shallow mind,' Hawkins prosed on, avoiding my eyes in case he erupted laughing. 'Which is understandable in the case of young Makepeace perhaps –' Young Makepeace tried to hit him and failed. I shoved him instead.

'Look.' I went back to Granny and Pope. 'What paraplegics lack is – sensation. Surely you can understand that? We're missing out with half our bodies. So the other half needs more. We need a lot of time to look and smell and *feel*.'

It didn't seem to make much impression.

'Well,' Granny was as tart as rhubarb, 'it'll probably rain when we have our trip to Weston. So you two will be pleased even if it's ruined for the rest of us.'

Mr Pope howled as Dennis ran a wheel against his foot.

'Blasted kids!' he yelped.

Hawkins nodded sagely. 'I couldn't agree more, Mr Pope.'

It had been marvellous at Clevedon. We'd gone on Sunday morning and listened to the church bells and watched the promenaders taking dogs and children for airings. The tide had been right out revealing an ugly muddy nudity that we had found vulnerable and appealing. We ran our chairs down the ramp and on to the slipway to Aunt Nell's horror.

'What would have happened if you'd gone off the edge?' she asked later, still a bit trembly as she served lunch.

'We'd have hit the rock and the headlines,' Hawkins told her.

She said, 'Oh, Luke . . .'

It was two weeks since our Fête day and he was fully 'integrated' into our peculiar society. Occasionally there would be times when he was silent and morose; not often. When he'd had a lousy session in physio and couldn't manage his new legs, that was the worst. He still refused to see his family; he said he wanted to be able to stand without crutches for their first visit.

In the afternoon Uncle Roger and Aunt Nell pushed us along cliff footpaths up a hilly headland where there was an old church and a graveyard full of leaning headstones. We rested and looked at the grey sea and the gulls wheeling and screaming around a cluster of rocks. Aunt Nell and Uncle Roger sat down so that they were on a level with us. They smiled and fought for breath. Hawkins talked about the gulls and some ducks he'd seen on the way up. It seemed they should be nearer fresh water.

I said, 'I like it here. I'd like to be put here when I die.'

Aunt Nell reached for a laugh and Uncle Roger panted, 'Fine. I'll keep a place next to me.'

Hawkins didn't say a word. He flashed me a look, which I couldn't identify, then his eyes seemed to go cold and opaque. Later, as we coasted back down the hill ahead of the mere pedestrians, he said tensely, 'Don't ever say things like that again, Fanny. It's not funny.'

'What isn't?' I knew. His prolonged silence told me. He didn't bother to enlighten me. I blustered. 'We all have to go you know, Hawkins.'

'Not for ages. And it's not funny.'

He sounded so mad that I didn't mention the fact that I hadn't been joking or trying to create an effect. We reached the bottom of the hill and ran our chairs on to brittle grass, turned and waited for the others.

I said suddenly, 'I'm sorry. It won't happen again.'

I had one of those strange feelings of premonition. He was silent for ages then he said, 'I wish Roger would hold Nell's hand or something.'

I glanced up as they came down the cliff path single file.

'It's not that steep.'

'No. I just wish – sometimes – he'd . . . hold her hand.'

I thought he was changing the subject and that my premonition had been a mistake. I thought he was a little embarrassed by his own intensity and his remark was a way of keeping his distance. And I told myself that was what I wanted. My job was to needle him into walking again and then he'd go home and I wouldn't see him any more. I didn't look properly at Uncle Roger and Aunt Nell.

The outing to Weston dawned breezy but cloudless. We went in two coaches with limited seating and plenty of space for our chairs.

Mr Pope said, 'It'll be blowing half a gale along the sea front. You see.'

Casey tucked a rug over his knees and checked he had his indigestion pills. 'The forecast is that the wind will drop, Mr Pope. I don't really think you need your winter overcoat.'

He held on to it grimly as if he expected her to rip it from his back. 'Oh yes I do. It's always windy at Weston. Even when it's sultry everywhere else.'

'Blow the cobwebs away then, won't it?' Granny cackled at him with her Jap officer teeth and opened her bag for me to see a stock of chocolate already disintegrating under pressure. I laughed – I hadn't done anything but laugh since I got up – and she cackled again and dug old Pope in the ribs.

We got to Weston and he was right, it was blowing a Force Nine all along the fine-sand beaches. Our helpers had to pull us along in reverse to avoid silting us up; as it was you could still taste the grittiness on your tongue and feel it beneath your eyelashes. We went early to the hotel where we'd booked luncheon and spent ages over it. Afterwards the oldies went to a cinema, the youngsters to the fun fair.

Hardly anyone was there. It was right on the end of the Grand Pier and everything creaked and groaned in the wind and looked desolate. The fair people were delighted to see us. They lifted us in and out of the bumper cars, settled us securely on the wooden horses, strapped us into the figure-of-eight carriages.

Hawkins bowled up to the man in charge of the Big Wheel.

'Can me and my girl have a ride? We've got thirty pence.'

The rides were plainly marked twenty pence each, but the man beamed at us and stopped the Wheel. I hardly noticed being lifted in and clamped down with the safety bar. Hawkins had called me his girl.

At the top of the circle we could see right over Weston. There was the enormous bay, fast filling with sea, the donkeys still battling gallantly along the sands, chip papers blowing on the prom. It was the most beautiful sight I had ever seen. I gasped and screamed little screams, and Hawkins put his arm along the back of the car and laughed with me. And then I lifted my face ecstatically.

'It's raining!' I called. 'It's raining –' The sky was grey but cloudless and not a spot marked the scoured promenade.

'So it is!' yelled Hawkins without even a lifted eyebrow. He tightened his arm and pulled me close against him. 'It's pouring. Pouring!'

We swept to ground level and had a quick vision of the man in charge gaping at us in amazement, then we climbed up again and left the mechanical racket far below us. The wind whipped my hair into Hawkins's face and he went on laughing through it. 'We'll drown,' I gasped into the wind.

'No we won't. I've got you. I'll hold you up.'

There was confidence in his voice. More than confidence, a masculine boastfulness. I looked round at him and stopped pumping out laughter. His eyes were striped grey and blue, his mobile mouth parted and grimaced against the gale. We stared. Then he kissed me.

'Fanny,' he breathed against my lips. 'Sweet Fanny Adams.'

For once I said nothing. I was nothing. Only what Lucas Hawkins made me.

Beamish sat on the corner of his desk and looked at me with his round eyes.

'I'm speaking to you as a friend, Fran. Not as a doctor. As a friend.'

'Okay.' I felt sick.

'Roger Parrish would say the same thing.'

'What about Aunt Nell? She wouldn't. She *trusts* me.'

'So do I, Fran. But you're only sixteen.'

'And never been kissed,' I quoted, trying desperately to sound flippant. And it wasn't true. I had been kissed . . . I had . . . I had. I made a supreme effort to change the subject. 'Which reminds me. How are you making out with Casey these days?'

He took a breath then let it out, capitulating.

'Fran, if you were a sixteen-year-old girl with legs that worked I would probably tell you to mind your own business at this precise moment.' He smiled very slightly to take the sting out of his words. 'So . . . mind your own business.'

I smiled too, well pleased with his reply. 'If it *was* my business because I happened to think a great deal of the two

109

parties concerned, I would be very happy with that answer, Brother Beamish. It tells me a lot.'

'You are incorrigible!' He gasped a laugh and jabbed a long finger at me. 'But you've given me my reason for telling you to go easy with Luke Hawkins. It's not because this is a Residential Home with rules and regulations. But because I think a great deal of the two parties concerned.'

The subject hadn't changed.

He'd met me as I came out of physio and I had known something was on his mind. He'd walked along to his office as he chatted about my sensation-increase, and I'd had to go with him. Then he'd suggested quietly that Luke and I were becoming 'too exclusive'. I couldn't take him seriously at first, it was such a crazy description of Luke and me. Even when he'd said, 'I'm speaking to you as a friend,' I was too euphoric to absorb it properly. I'd just started to feel sick. Now I knew how serious he was. He was relating his feeling for Casey to Luke's for me. He was taking *us* very seriously indeed.

I blurted defensively, 'You started it. You and Uncle Roger and Aunt Nell. Weeks ago before I was ill. You thought I might be able to use my feminine wiles to −'

He leaned forward suddenly and took my hands in both of his. I realized then that they had been fighting the air in protest; sketching an invisible wall between us.

'Fran. Dear Fran.'

He stilled me with that magic touch of his. His hands knew mine. Used to probing the human skeleton through its barrier of flesh and skin and nerve ends, his phalanges locked on mine and held me still. He kept looking at me until I looked back at him honestly. Then he spoke very quietly indeed.

'You love him, don't you?'

Tears flooded my eyes. I had tried hard *not* to analyse

what I felt for Luke Hawkins, simply to enjoy it. Now I knew there was no need for analysis. I loved him. This was what love was. All the reading I had done was useless and stupid and completely misleading. Love play. The French kiss. Orgasms. Things that could never be for me because I had no feeling below hip level. They were nothing. Nothing. Nothing. Because without them I could still love. With my mind and soul. And with my body. My pulsating, beating body.

Beamish whispered insidiously, 'Then you know, Fran. You know you cannot hurt him.'

I swallowed my tears. 'He loves me too!' It sounded like a cry for help in the sunlit dust-moted room.

'Does he? Is he as . . . committed . . . as you are Fran?'

I had asked for help and he had given me . . . that. He was asking me whether Hawkins would have looked twice at me if his legs were still there. I began to shake but I spoke very clearly nonetheless.

'And if not, what do you propose? A mild flirtation?' I tried to free my hands, unsuccessfully. 'Just enough to get him going so that he'll keep trying with his tin legs? Maybe I should let him touch me up a bit? After all I couldn't feel a thing and if he could get through my plastic pants and the sani pads it might give him a bit of a thrill!'

His grip hurt like hell.

He said levelly, 'Stop hurting yourself, Fran – d'you hear me? Stop it!' He breathed twice, very deeply then went on, 'Luke will walk now, Fran. You've done that for him – given him motivation. Given him back his interest in life. Now, let's take it from there. If you go on as you are, you will become indispensable to him. So that . . . afterwards . . . he will be back to square one. Feeling life has cheated him all over again. Can't you see that?'

I whispered, 'Afterwards?'

'That's what I said Fran.'

I did not take my eyes from his face and my hands gripped his in return. So we stayed for a long time. Then I whispered again, 'If we could have a year . . . maybe two . . . I could let him down gently.'

He just shook his head.

I don't remember getting up to my room. Zeek and Dorothy watched me as I wept. I couldn't stop.

CHAPTER FOURTEEN

Luke said, 'Fanny. You're not ill are you?' There was sudden panic in his voice.

'I'm not ill. I want to be quiet. Is that a crime?'

'It's against nature where you're concerned. I have just told you that Granny and Pope are having it off in the summerhouse, and you told me to shut *up*?'

Just for a moment the thought of Granny and Pope having it off in the summerhouse got through to me and I ghosted a smile.

'Oh Hawkins . . . shut up.'

'Okay. But Aunt Nell will be here any moment and if you tell her to shut up she'll bleed inside.'

It was Sunday. I'd gone to wait on the horseshoe lawn for the Parrishes' station wagon. Not that I intended to ask for advice or anything like that, but Aunt Nell and Uncle Roger would be a shield between me and Hawkins. The real me and the real Hawkins. And then he'd joined me.

'I'm not about to tell Aunt Nell to shut up. Uncle Roger wouldn't let me anyway.'

'He's not coming.'

'How do you know?'

'I rang him.' Hawkins sounded suddenly evasive.

I said sharply, 'Why?'

'Can't remember what he said . . . business meeting I think.'

'Why did you ring him?' I pursued grimly.

The station wagon rolled through the gates closely followed by a navy-blue Daimler.

Hawkins smiled. 'I wanted to let him know he'd be meeting my parents this afternoon. I didn't want you to feel out on a limb or anything. But Aunt Nell can cope. She's bought a new dress specially.'

I was silent for a long time, staring at him. Along the edge of my vision the two cars crawled towards the house. Aunt Nell was going about two miles an hour so that she could wave to us.

He said nervously, 'Don't look at me like that, Fran. It was what you wanted. For me to get together with my parents again. I thought you'd be pleased.'

I blurted rudely, 'I don't want to meet them. I'm going to my room.'

'Fanny – you can't!' He manoeuvred his chair clumsily against mine. The wheels clashed. In full view of the house and the cars he put his arms around me. 'The whole idea is for them to meet you! Darling Fanny – you're not scared of anything! They're just people!'

I said monotonously, 'I must go to my room.' But he wouldn't release my arms so that I could reach the wheels and then Aunt Nell came galloping towards us like the American marines to the rescue. Her smile was wide but anxious and she draped her arms around the two of us in an effort to make our embrace look less exclusive. Beamish's word again. We must not be exclusive.

'Isn't this marvellous?' Her hand held my shoulder tightly, protectively. 'Mr and Mrs Hawkins are here! It's a real party! Let's go and meet them and take them into the games room, shall we? It's rather cold out here and you've not got your cardigan, Frances, dear.'

The Weston wind had seeped up-channel and shook the aspen as she spoke. I shivered.

They were both tall and big; outdoor people. They wore identical macs against the threatened rain, khaki coloured and voluminous and tatty in a frightfully posh way. They greeted Luke with a deliberate lack of emotion, Mr Hawkins shaking his hand vigorously, Mrs giving him her cheek without letting any other part of her body touch his. They both shook my hand and said heartily they'd heard a great deal about me. Mr kept my hand in his and patted the back of it. Mrs said, 'We've a great deal to thank you for, Frances. Mrs Parrish has been telling us –'

Aunt Nell interrupted nervously, 'We had a little chat before we left, Frances, dear. I – I put Luke's parents in the picture. About Thornton Hall.'

I glanced at her, appalled that she was frightened of me. Her blue eyes were pleading. I saw that the new dress was fit for a wedding; pure silk with a matching coat. I was terrified I was going to cry so I took her hand and rubbed my face into the palm in a childish gesture that immediately reassured Mr and Mrs Hawkins. Aunt Nell looked surprised and then, as she felt the dampness, she became very bright.

'Shall we lead the way, Fran . . .' She pushed me over the turf so that we were ahead of the others. It was the first time she had pushed my chair. I found my handkerchief and scrubbed at my face.

Mr Hawkins drew up chairs next to the billiard table.

'This will book it for later,' he chuckled. 'Though whether I can still beat Luke from this low level . . .'

Luke said, 'Give yourself the same handicap as me, Dad. Play from a chair.'

Mrs Hawkins flushed painfully and pressed back against the edge of the table. She was as flat as a board and skinny

115

in a sinewy tough way. I smiled at Aunt Nell squatting close to my chair like a mother hen. How beautiful she was.

Luke took an enormous breath.

'Well. I told you about Fanny on the phone. She likes to be called Fran, by the way, by everybody except me.' He grinned at me but I wasn't reassured. He was making us exclusive again. 'I told you how she practically forced me to take part in the entertainment we did on Fête day –'

'I do wish you'd let us come to that, old son. We'd have enjoyed seeing you get your accolade –'

'No one knew I'd done anything, Dad. It was a secret. Anyway then Fanny and I started to meet –'

'Secretly?' asked Mrs Hawkins, eyes opening wide.

'Of course. That was the whole *point* . . . anyway, then we went to Mrs Parrish's house for the day and then to Weston on our outing. And we realized we were meant for each other. That's what the whole thing is about.'

We all stared at him. How can you feel sick and proud at the same time. I felt sick and proud at the same time. Aunt Nell looked proud. Mr and Mrs Hawkins bewildered. Luke waved his hands at them impatiently.

'I mean, that's why I pranged that bike! Why the paper mills make so much lucre! Why – why the universe *is*!'

Mr Hawkins was the first to recover. He laughed a rumbly, comfortable, unflappable laugh.

'I think our young man is in love, Marion,' he said to his wife.

Luke said, 'Well done, Dad. Top marks.'

Mrs Hawkins said, 'I can't quite . . . you met . . . face to face . . . on the Fête day. Is that right?'

'Two weeks before then.' Luke spoke with a studied patience that was insulting. 'Then we kept away. I wanted to surprise Fanny by coming to the show on my legs and there was a lot of work to be done. I couldn't have managed without Nell and Roger of course. I can still only do six steps –'

'And the Fête day was July the twenty-sixth. Four and a half weeks ago. You've known each other four and a half weeks.'

'My God, Mother! We've always known each other! We practically *recognized* each other! Can't you under*stand*?'

In spite of everything – incredibly – my heart lifted, bounded, inside me. Beamish had been wrong in one thing. Hawkins felt as I felt. He was as committed as I was.

Aunt Nell leaned forward. 'Mrs Hawkins – Mr Hawkins – there's no explaining it. If you can come and see them often, you will be reassured. Frances will tell you how – how conventional – how cautious, I am. Yet when you are with them you know they are right for each other.'

What was she saying?

Suddenly Mrs Hawkins was all up-tight. 'Of course, you have had the opportunity to be with them and witness this – er – relationship develop.'

'Yes, old son. It's rather hurtful to your mother and me that you have shut us out so completely. Until now.'

Somehow Luke controlled himself. I watched him swallow that fiery temper of his while Aunt Nell stammered something placating.

Then he spread his hands, palms up.

'Look, Mum. Dad. I'm sorry. I behaved badly. But I thought you understood. I had to find my own way. Or die. I admit I wanted to die. At least I thought that was what I wanted –'

Both the Hawkinses stumbled over their swift reassurance; Mrs Hawkins got off her chair and crouched by the step of his, lightly touching his honeycomb blanket.

He took another breath. 'Surely you're not of the school that thinks because I've lost my legs I can't get married.'

We were all thrown back again by the blast; except Nell. She still stooped among her silken draperies, smiling as if this was all completely normal.

Luke nodded emphatically. 'That's why I wanted to see you. Fanny and I are going to get married.'

I should have said immediately, 'First time I've heard of it.' Anything. But I sat there, surely with a nimbus of light around me. Me. Married.

'Now look, old son. Frances is sixteen. You're eighteen –'

'The age of consent!' Luke twitched his shoulders. 'Oh God. We'll wait if we have to. But why do we have to? Why waste time?'

At last Aunt Nell did what Uncle Roger would have done half an hour ago.

'Your parents are simply pleased to see you Luke . . . and to meet Frances of course. Now, you've announced your intentions, so why not leave it until next week? Perhaps Mrs Hawkins would like to play Frances at table tennis while you and your father –'

Hawkins wouldn't let it drop just like that of course.

'Okay. But I want Fanny to see the house, Dad. So that we can plan some alterations – ramps and things like that. When can you come and fetch us?'

He was so gloriously single-minded. So blindly selfish.

Mr Hawkins, still seeing me as a little girl, said indulgently, 'We'll have to see how Frances feels about that, won't we? You're very quiet my dear. Question of still waters run deep, I expect. What do you think about Luke's plans?'

They all looked at me expectantly. Now was the time. I

kept my eyes on Mr Hawkins, terrified they would stray to Luke. Now was the time. Now. Absolutely *now*.

I said in a monotone, 'I don't want to get married. I couldn't leave Thornton Hall. I need drugs. And – and I wet my knickers. Often. I couldn't get married. I couldn't leave Thornton Hall.'

I saw the Hawkinses relax. I saw Aunt Nell and Luke thrown back, as incredulous as I had been a moment before. In that precious time I had my chair turned and was out of the games room and down the hall. Luke gave a cry and a female voice said, 'Let her go dear, she needs to be on her own . . .' and I had another few seconds to charge the ramp and get into the lift. As I punched the button Aunt Nell appeared in the hall.

'Fran – wait –' her face was agonized. The doors closed and I was up and out and in my room and Zeek was locked behind me. When she knocked two minutes later I had myself in hand.

'Aunt Nell . . .' I called through the solid oak. 'Please fob them off somehow. I'll explain later. Please help me. I can't see Luke – not for a while.'

She must have leaned against Zeek regaining her breath after the stairs. I could imagine her lovely dress draping her ample curves . . . I felt terrible.

At last she said, 'All right, dear. All right. I do understand really. You're so young and this is all so unexpected. But Frances, dear . . . don't be afraid. Please don't be afraid. This isn't frightening at all . . . it's wonderful.'

I wept silently. I remembered how buttoned-up she'd been when she met me last June. It was amazing what love could do. I wept again.

CHAPTER FIFTEEN

Two days later. It was September the first and amazingly summer had gone. While I sat up here in my dormer there had been several storms which had lashed the flowers relentlessly. If Hawkins and I had been at Clevedon, Aunt Nell would have let us go out in it – I knew she would.

Casey gave her special knock and I went over and unlocked Zeek. She came in carrying a milky drink as if my two day incarceration and Luke's subsequent uproar were the norm.

She said, 'You missed physio again. Miss Hamlin is furious.'

I couldn't find the energy to say the obvious: that Miss Hamlin was never furious.

Casey said, 'Are you all right?'

'Yes.'

'You'll have to see him some time.'

'Why?'

'Well, how long are you going to live up here like this? Why won't you see the others? Granny has been up twice.'

'I know. I heard her hammering and calling.'

'Well then?'

I replied with my own kind of logic. 'It wouldn't be fair to let Granny in and not Hawkins.'

She put away a few things, stirred the drink, placed it on

a little tray that clipped to my chair, and clipped the tray into place.

'I thought you might feel that way. But in any case, you're not being fair to him, are you?'

'This is the best way, Casey — and you know it. If I tell him to clear off he'll argue and argue . . . he's so stubborn.' I looked at my drink and shuddered. 'This way, he'll eventually get the message. He'll go home and sulk. I know him.' Immediately she'd gone I'd swill the drink down the loo.

She sat on the bed. Casey sat on the *bed*.

'That's not the point, Fran. He deserves an explanation.'

I looked at her and she looked right back at me very steadily.

I breathed, 'You know. You've known all along.'

She shrugged. 'Naturally. I'm your special nurse. I have to know your clinical details.'

'But you've never said . . . you treat me as if I'm normal.'

'Which you are.' She made a flat impatient gesture with her hand. 'Fran, just for once, you're not seeing straight. You don't know when you're going to die any more than I know. We're here now. At this moment. That's all we really *know*.' Her eyes were so intensely blue they dazzled mine. I blinked.

'I don't want Luke on those terms. He'd feel bound to be gentle . . . kind . . . We're not like that.'

She grinned. 'You can say that again!' She shook her head. 'I'm not thinking of you and Luke at this moment, Fran. Just you. Stop being frightened. You're you and you're here. Just as I'm me and I'm here.'

I genuinely tried. But I wasn't just me any more. I was me and Luke. I shook my head blindly.

'All right then.' She sighed and stood up. 'Back to Luke.

He deserves to know about this Fran. If you're talking about being fair – that is fair. Hide away afterwards if you must, but tell him.'

'You think he'll talk me into . . . into . . . something.'

She tapped her foot.

'I haven't got time to chatter like this. Drink your drink. I have to take the cup straight back down.'

I nearly choked getting the glucosed milk down my throat. She stood by unrelentingly until every last little drop was gone. Then she said, 'By the way, we want you to be the first to know. Douglas and I. We're getting married.'

I looked up at her. White cap like a halo on golden hair; strawberries and cream complexion, speedwell blue eyes, full – but firm – mouth.

I clenched my hands to stop the tears. 'When?' I asked.

'I forgot you'd want it cut and dried. The actual date has not been fixed.'

'Make it soon,' I advised.

'Why?'

I raised my brows in imitation of my old self. 'Because of me. I'm still here – I heard you say so. And Beamish thinks I'm a mermaid.'

For an awful minute I thought she would cry. Then she turned to Zeek. 'Luke's waiting for you under the aspen, Fran. When he isn't badgering Beamish or Bennie or knocking on Zeek or trying to get your phone reconnected, he's waiting on that damned lawn. Whatever his reaction, he should know. And you should tell him.'

I bit my lip on the same old place and tasted blood.

'Seriously, I can't see him, Casey. I'd hang on to him and beg him never to leave me. I can't do that to him.'

'Why not?'

'Oh, *Casey* . . .' I jerked my chair over to the window.

'Look . . . get my phone plugged back in, will you? I'll compromise. I'll phone him. It's how it all started and it might as well finish that way.'

She hesitated, then gave in. 'All right.' Maybe she thought Luke would persuade me out into the garden to hear the nightingales.

She opened Zeek.

'Thanks for the congratulations and best wishes,' she mentioned. 'Douglas will be as thrilled as I am.'

I smiled. She would be so *good* for Beamish. It was the one decent thing I'd accomplished at Thornton Hall.

I rang him just before midnight as usual.

He said, 'Thank Christ. I want to kill you, d'you know that? What the hell d'you think you're playing at? Or is that how you see it – as a game? And when you see it's getting serious, you back down. Is that it?'

'Something like that.'

'Sod it, Fanny. It's something else. No one can get at you – Granny – Stella. I know what's happening – I can read you like a book. D'you think I care about wet knickers?'

'Ever smelt 'em?'

'Fanny you just won't understand will you? I want to share everything with you. Everything. My aching stumps. Your wet knickers.' He tried to laugh and it was a sob. 'Fanny Adams . . . I can't live without you.'

I squeezed my eyes tight shut.

'Hawkins. You'll have to. Start learning now.'

There was something in my voice that stopped him. I could hear him breathing jerkily. He said at last, 'I thought you felt as I do. I *know* you do. Dammit Fanny, I want the truth.'

Casey was right. He deserved that.

123

I said carefully, 'Listen. Listen hard, Hawkins, because I'm not going to repeat myself and this is the end of the conversation. I've got a dicky heart. I've always known about it and I know I'm living on borrowed time right now. Beamish thinks it will be soon. I'm going to have to rest a lot. No excitement. Sorry . . . sorry Hawkins. I shouldn't have let it . . . us . . . happen. I wish you'd go home now and let me be at peace. That's what I really want Hawkins. For you to go home.'

I put my finger on the receiver rest. Immediately it pinged that we were cut off, I let it go and laid the receiver on my table. It hummed emptily. He wouldn't be able to ring me back and the staff had been alerted to stop him coming up to my room.

I wondered how he felt. Perhaps there was a part of me that hoped he would force himself on me still; take me by storm.

The next afternoon Casey told me he had left. His parents had been sent for and he had moved out, bag and baggage.

CHAPTER SIXTEEN

Time passed. One day the dahlias were all blackened and the chrysanths looked as if they'd fall down if it weren't for Mr Ottwell's stakes. I watched him from my dormer as he went round nipping the dead blooms into a big plastic sack. He scorned secateurs. His horny thumb nail was as efficient and much kinder. Later he went behind the swimming pool where he had a slow, perpetual bonfire going. The cremation of the frosted dahlias was a sweet-scented affair; I opened my window and breathed it in with the sharp, cold, sun-filled Michaelmas air.

Next day it was the turn of the roses. Not all of them. Some, in the shelter of the protective box hedges, still bloomed fragilely. I wondered whether they wept for their burning companions.

Casey wheeled me down to physio against my will and Miss Hamlin slapped and pummelled me with even more energy than usual. When she rolled me over and pulled me up her face was bright red.

'Any more sensation, Fran?' she panted.

I shook my head. 'I don't know why you bother. You're wasting your time.'

She looked up at me. 'What?' She lifted her ribs for a gigantic breath. 'I've heard my job called a lot of things – sometimes I'm a torturer – but I'm never a time waster. How dare you insult me like that, Fran!'

I shrugged and leaned down to haul up my jeans.

'I suppose you're thinking of Rosie?'

Why should I think of Rosie Jimpson in her pram, smiling warmly at everyone as they coddled and petted her? And then I knew in a flash. I almost cried aloud with the pain of it. Rosie in her protected spot, would survive a little longer than some of us. Only a little.

Miss Hamlin said very quietly, her breathing controlled now, 'If you think any time spent with Rosie is wasted, then you're not seeing straight Fran.' She pulled socks over my feet and swung me into my chair. Her hand rested on my shoulder for a moment. A very strong hand, short-fingered and spatulate, with large knuckles and no ring marks. That afternoon I helped Rosie with yet another jigsaw puzzle. It was so boring she fell asleep in the middle of it like she always did. I didn't wheel away. When she woke up I'd started on the middle and left the straight edges for her. It didn't make me feel any better.

Beamish said, 'So you told him?'

'Yes.'

'Just like that. Straight out.'

'Was there any other way?'

'I should have thought so. You could have asked for his help.'

'We're not like that,' I said wearily, surely for the fiftieth time? 'We weren't like that. We were equal.'

'And you imagine that if you'd asked for his help, it would have made you unequal? Listen, Fran. I help you. Do you think you don't help me? Not just Casey, bless your heart, but all the time? We're equal . . . you *know* we are.'

'Thanks . . . thanks.' I meant it. But it was all too late, this bridging of the gap between them and us. It was too late because Luke had gone. 'Never mind now . . . just leave it.'

He left it.

'Listen, Fran. We thought – Linda and I – we thought we could take you out somewhere today. The downs perhaps or –'

'Linda?'

'Casey.'

'Is that her name?' I looked out of the window and frowned at the sun. 'Is it Sunday then?'

'Yes.'

A whole week since Luke had announced that we were going to be married. My frown deepened. A whole week since I had seen Aunt Nell.

'Thanks a lot, Beamish, but I'd counted on going to Clevedon today. The Parrishes will be here any minute now.'

He fiddled with something on his desk. 'Not today, Fran. Next week I expect. That's why Linda and I thought –'

'Is she ill? Is Aunt Nell ill, Beamish?'

'No –'

'Something's wrong. I know it is. She would have come before.'

'I think she feels she can no longer help you, Fran.'

Pain was everywhere. I said wildly, 'Are you trying to tell me she and Uncle Roger want to give me up?'

He picked up the phone. 'She is a reticent woman, Fran. When she felt she had something to offer, she came. Now she feels she has nothing. But if you telephoned – asked her to come –'

I swallowed convulsively. The habit of years dies hard even at sixteen. Yet I wanted Aunt Nell. I swallowed again and I think it must have been pride because I nodded.

Beamish dialled briskly. 'All right. Then I'll tell you. She asked me not to but I will anyway. Roger has left her. He's been playing around for years but always stayed with Nell. Now he's gone and she's alone.'

I reached for the phone and then I could hardly speak. I managed something like, 'Aunt Nell. Luke has gone and I need you. Please come and fetch me as soon as you can.'

She didn't speak for about three seconds. Then she whispered, 'I'll be with you in half an hour Fran. Ask Casey to pack an overnight bag.' And she put down the phone.

I stared at Beamish.

'I'm sorry. I can smell my pants. I must have wetted myself.'

So Nell and I were together for the next three days and we comforted each other. We behaved very normally. At eight o'clock she would run my bath and help me into it. Then she'd hover and try to help me while I slapped her hand away and gasped, 'I'm perfectly capable . . .' Then we'd have breakfast in the window overlooking the front; then we'd wash up and go out to shop for lunch. Sometimes we had fish and chips in newspaper and ate them on the slipway and drowsed half the afternoon away against the September-warm stone. Aunt Nell wanted it to go on always. She said, 'Fran, you can see we're managing. Why can't it last?'

'Because.' I smiled at her in case she was hurt.

'Because why?'

'Because I need to have somewhere to run to. This is the perfect place. If I have you all the time –'

'That's nonsense, Frances. And you know it.'

I smiled again and closed my eyes. I felt her hand on my arm and I put my other hand up and covered hers.

We didn't talk about Uncle Roger or Luke.

We had wintry teas in the window; muffins and jam and watercress sandwiches and Genoa cake and very hot strong tea with loads of sugar. It would get dark and we'd switch on the television and have the news and then we'd play cards or read or talk about our favourite things.

I told her I wanted to go out in the rain.

'Then you shall.' No arguments about catching pneumonia. 'The very next time you're here when it's raining, I'll come along the front with you.'

'Without an umbrella?'

'Without an umbrella.'

'There is one other thing. You'd never let me, of course. But it would be the best thing ever.'

She eyed me with suspicious blue eyes.

'Go on.'

'I'd . . . I'd like more than anything to swim in the channel.'

'Out there? In that murky water out there?'

'I'm a murky character myself, Aunt Nell. I'd be a real mermaid. A muddy mermaid.'

'Maybe next summer we could go down to Bude.'

'No good. Too nice. Too proper.' I jerked a thumb at the window. 'This is my sea. And I don't want the summer and the crowds gawking. I want to go in in the rain. When it's dark.'

She made a gigantic effort at a joke. 'You'll get awfully wet.' Then she said, 'Maybe . . . if I came with you . . . it's so crazy!'

I knew I'd won. I clasped her hand in both of mine. 'We'll be like Amy Johnson! Like the bloke who climbed Everest! Think how we'll *feel*!'

She didn't really understand of course, but she accepted it, like a mother accepts things. So then and there I told her everything. It all spilled out without any more reservations. Hanging on to her hand and looking into her face. I didn't know whether Beamish had already mentioned it. She didn't say anything; just listened. I told her how I'd heard a couple of nurses talking when I was ten. How I'd played them up all day pretending I was a princess. How – because I was left on those damned steps I used to pretend all the time I was someone famous. How I'd been ordering the nurses about and being unbearable and then how the one had said to the other – try to be patient – weak heart – respiratory difficulties – won't live past puberty. So then how I'd looked up the word puberty. And how when I got to be fifteen I thought I'd scored over the nurses and God. How they'd offered me a place at Thornton Hall and I knew Thornton Hall was expensive and the Social Services wouldn't pay for me to go there indefinitely. So how that first night I'd asked Beamish and he told me that diagnoses were proved wrong every day. So I knew then that there wasn't much time. I told her how I knew this with one part of me but that there were other parts that wouldn't believe my head. Until Beamish warned me to go easy on Luke. And then . . . oh yes, right then . . . I knew with all of me.

Aunt Nell listened. It took me ages to say it all, nearly an hour. She didn't interrupt. At the end I expected her to nag me to come and live with her. She didn't. She sighed and released my hands and got up to switch on the light and pull the curtains.

Then at last she spoke.

'It's still not in the least cold, is it, Fran?' she asked. 'Next weekend, whether it rains or not, we'll take that swim.'

I said hoarsely, 'Thanks, Aunt Nell.'

Somehow Thursday and Friday went and it was Saturday and Aunt Nell was coming. Casey said it was colder so

I wore a sweater and packed another one. I managed to sneak my swimming costume in my case without her seeing. There was fruit on the breakfast table and I ate a banana and swallowed it carefully. I wasn't worried about my lack of appetite any more. I would eat with Aunt Nell.

At ten o'clock she hadn't come. I went back upstairs and found Casey making my bed.

'I was going to do that,' I lied. I hadn't done it since my last day with Hawkins. 'I thought the cleaners were doing it anyway.'

She went on working, flapping out a fresh sheet, slapping it under the mattress at the bottom, doing neat envelope sides.

'You don't get the cleaners coming in,' she reminded me. 'Anyway I had something for you.'

'What?'

She nodded her head at Zeek's inside. I looked. An enormous willow grew up his middle and cascaded its fronds around my flowers.

'Hey!' I was open-mouthed with admiration. 'Casey! It's terrific! Where did you get it?'

'Wallpaper. Debenhams. Saw it last week and bought a roll yesterday. Thought it would fill in the top half.'

The treacherous tears were there again. I managed to say, 'Casey. It's beautiful. Thanks.'

'My pleasure.' She picked up the laundry bag and made for the door. 'Have a good weekend.'

I wanted to tell her about the swim. I wanted to tell her much more than that. But she was gone.

At eleven I rang Beamish and asked him to phone Aunt Nell's number for me. He rang back to say there was no answer so she must be on her way. I held Dorothy on my lap and looked at the willow. Cricket bats are made of willow because it is so pliant and can absorb shocks. Weeping willow.

At twelve I stuffed Dorothy on top of my case and went downstairs to wait for Aunt Nell. No one was about. I went into the lounge and spoke to the dogs. They rolled on their backs and their tongues fell out of their open mouths on to the floor. A clatter of dishes came from the dining-room; a desultory tap-tap of a ping-pong ball from the games room. I opened the doors and pushed out on to the terrace. Clouds were massing up in the west and I wondered whether it would rain. Far down the ribbon of the drive, a car appeared driving very slowly; the station wagon. I waved fruitlessly and bowled my chair down the ramp and on to the lawn, weak with relief. I was behind the box hedge. I stopped and lifted myself on my arms to call again to Aunt Nell as she pulled up. Then I sat down again. Uncle Roger was driving the station wagon. And beside him, his leonine fair head as angry as ever, was Lucas Hawkins.

I did not know what to do. I cowered in my chair with my heart hitting my ribs and my stomach sick with fear. The car door slammed. Someone came out of the house; there were low voices. The rear doors squeaked and there were the usual clicking sounds of a chair being unfolded. Then wheels on the gravel. Then the front door closed.

I put my head on my stupid knees and wondered why the world would not end then and there. When I raised my head the garden swam around and then flowed through me like a river. I jerked my wheels and got on the lawn and made for the aspen tree as if Aunt Nell might somehow be there waiting for me all the time. I could hear someone calling her name. 'Nell! Nell!' My chair was beneath the umbrella of whispering leaves and it was my own voice calling. I tipped my head back as far as it would go and fought to exhale properly before I sucked in more air. I wanted to faint . . . yet I strove to stay conscious.

Uncle Roger walked across the lawn alone. He wore his grey flannels but no white shirt; a heavy-knit sweater instead. He crouched by my chair.

'Hello, Fran.' He covered my hand. 'Hello. Hello Fran.'

I looked at him. The sound of the restless aspen leaves entered my ears and filled my brain with their murmuring. There was no wind. Yet there must be. I could hear the sea. The murky grey sea where tonight Aunt Nell and I would swim like mermaids.

'Won't you speak to me, Fran?'

I looked at him and heard the leaves like the sea and it would allow nothing else in my head.

'Fran. Whatever you think of me, I love you. Will you believe that? Just nod. Just tell me you believe that.'

Nell. Nell was left on the steps. Because she was barren.

'I have to tell you, Fran. I have to tell you. There's no way I can make it easy. Oh God, Fran . . . Nell's gone. Nell's drowned.'

I didn't speak. The aspen leaves: the sea: they were loud.

'You've got to accept it, Fran. Her body was found this morning. On the beach.'

A wave crashed somewhere and in the aftermath of silence I said loudly, 'No.'

My voice seemed to reassure him. He began to talk rapidly in short cut-off sentences. A picture emerged: I shut my eyes and fought against it but it grew with his every word. The police at the top of the slipway where we had been sitting four days ago. Under the strings of dead fairy lights, an ambulance, its blue light flashing. Men in thigh-high fishermen's wellingtons lifting her off the rocks and putting her on the stretcher.

I looked at Uncle Roger again. He had dropped his head

and was staring at the indefatigable daisies. Did he know it was my fault? Did he know about tonight's swim?

He said dully, 'Of course, Fran, you know I'd left her so it's no good pretending with you, is it? I'll never forgive myself . . . but she was so level-headed, how could I know – how could I know Fran – that she would do this?'

He looked up. His grey eyes were pleading. For a long moment I was still silent, wanting him to be hurt, telling myself he deserved to be hurt. Then through the sea and the aspen leaves I heard birdsong and I remembered that Aunt Nell had loved him.

I said slowly, 'You think she drowned herself deliberately? Because you had left her? Because she couldn't have children?'

He flinched as if I'd hit him, then sat back on his heels.

'She told you she couldn't have children?'

'She told me nothing –' I couldn't bear this. I had to get away quickly.

He whispered, 'It would have been like her. It's me . . . oh God . . .'

Everything seemed to be waiting. The aspen held its breath.

'You . . .' I breathed. 'You're . . . impotent.'

It was a word I had read but never spoken. As it emerged into the stillness it had an awfulness of its own. Impotent. I remembered looking it up. 'Wanting in physical, mental or intellectual powers.' It described me. And Uncle Roger. Not Aunt Nell. Aunt Nell had been fully potent. She had had all her powers. And she had used them to protect . . . us.

He didn't speak and his flush deepened but he did not drop his gaze. I leaned back in the chair and closed my eyes. I knew why Aunt Nell had loved him. I told him the truth for her sake.

'It was nothing to do with you.' I whispered still, but my words were perfectly clear. 'She did not kill herself – we were going swimming tonight, the two of us. She promised. She was trying it out–'

'You're not making sense, Fran –'

'Then you're not listening.' I opened my eyes. 'It was one of my crazy ideas – surely you can believe that? And I persuaded her . . . so last night, being Aunt Nell . . . she had to try it first.'

He said, 'She was wearing her costume certainly.'

I could imagine her. Folding her clothes neatly in her room. Steeling herself. She hadn't wanted to do it. She had done it for me. Had those big shoulders been very much bruised? And had she been frightened? I couldn't take it . . .

Uncle Roger's hands enclosed my face. His grey eyes were as clear as pools.

'Listen, Fran.' His voice was urgent. 'Try to imagine how thankful Nell must have been. When she knew . . . when she knew she wasn't going to make it. At least she knew . . . she knew she had saved you from drowning.'

I stared up at him. He had come out of his own misery and touched mine. He understood. He hadn't fooled me after all. This was his real gift. That he understood.

I heard that bird singing again just as across the lawn Casey came running, her beautiful face stretched tight across her cheek bones.

'Fran – Fran – are you all right?'

Her cap was gone and her beautiful golden hair tumbled over my face as we held each other and wept.

CHAPTER SEVENTEEN

They told me that Luke was waiting for me on my corridor.

Casey said, 'D'you want to rest in my room for a while, Fran? Or shall I stay with you?'

I shook my head. 'What will Uncle Roger do now?'

She said, 'He has a great deal to do. Don't think about it.'

'He brought Luke here. Has Luke to go away with him?'

'No. Luke is back in his old room. Roger went there first to tell Luke and Luke decided to come back to Thornton Hall.'

I grinned crookedly. 'To hold my hand.'

She thought I was bitter. 'What is wrong with that, Fran?' she asked straightly.

'Nothing. Nothing at all, Casey.'

The lift doors opened and he was sitting in his wheel-chair outside Zeek. He stayed where he was. I went to him slowly.

I said, 'She didn't drown herself you know, Luke.'

He watched me. His eyes were very stripy and looked smaller than I remembered. Had he been crying a lot too?

'I didn't think she could have. Not Nell.'

'She promised me we'd go swimming tonight. When it was dark.'

He got all the implications. He said steadily, 'She was inclined to be quixotic, was Nell.'

I made a noise in my throat. 'Yes.'

He said, 'This would please her. A lot.'

Another noise. Was it hiccoughs? 'What?'

'Us. Here. Together.'

I said violently, 'If you're trying to say because she's drowned we've got to pick everything up where we left it –'

'Don't be so bloody stupid.' But he didn't sound angry at all. Calm and very certain. He smiled slightly. 'I mean what I said. Whether she were alive or dead. It would please her to know that we are together.'

A wave of pure sadness separate from the awfulness of Nell – grief swept from my waist upwards.

'Oh Luke. We can't go back. Too much has happened. All that – it's over. We were children playing in the sun.'

'I agree. Now . . . now we go on. The blindfolds are off, Fanny. No more games. We go on.'

'How? Like Granny and Pope? Bickering over the menus?'

'Yes. Of course. And like Casey and Beamish. And like Nell and Roger even. There's so many ways to love Fanny. We're going to do 'em all . . .'

I said again, without hope, 'How?'

He said, 'Give me the key to Zeek.'

I fumbled in my tidy bag and handed the key over. It was all so futile. There was nothing left.

He unlocked Zeek and pushed him wide. Then he swivelled his chair and faced me.

'Watch this Fanny.'

I watched.

He took the rug from his waist. He wore jeans and at the end of the jeans were black shoes. Slowly, smiling at me, he leaned down and pushed his left shoe over to his right and tucked the step of his chair out of the way. Then he knocked his left leg to the ground and followed it with his right. He sat up and placed his hands on the arms of his chair. Then he shoved. A grunt came from him and he stopped smiling, but he was up. He was standing free of the chair. He had no sticks, no crutches. He was free. Hawkins was free.

He took two swinging, jerky steps towards me and leaned down.

'No!' I gasped. 'No – Luke – you can't do it – you'll hurt yourself.'

'Shut up, Fanny, will you?'

His left arm was round my shoulders, his right lifting my useless knees. Our faces were close and I could see the sweat on his. He heaved mightily and I left my chair. Like a weight-lifter he rested, his face contorted. I flung my arms round his neck trying to throw my own weight with that next gargantuan effort. A noise, half groan, half shout of triumph came from him. We were up.

He rolled to the left, then to the right. He staggered and leaned against Zeek's jamb. I focused on the first flower I had ever stuck to the oak; a forget-me-not. And then Hawkins pushed himself upright again.

We crossed the threshold.

CONCLUSION

by Lucas Hawkins

Frances Adamson died on the ninth December two years ago.

I see she gave no description of herself. She was dark with very fluffy hair that sprang out of her head and would never lie flat. Her eyes were brown and very large. It was true she could resemble a marmoset. Also a bird. She was very small and fragile and along the backs of her beautiful hands and on her temples, there was a tracery of fine blue veins. If her legs had 'worked' – as she always put it – she would have been a dancer. As it was she enjoyed a curious kinship with objects and humans around her and she was constantly 'interpreting' them, much as a dancer 'interprets' music and movement.

Her spirit and her sense of fun were limitless. Before she died she insisted she wished to be buried next to Aunt Nell in the cemetery above the sea, wearing her mermaid's tail. She said it mischievously and quite without solemnity. We laughed about it. But it was arranged.

A week after she finished writing, I took her to my parents' home and for a while she was happy to be cloistered there with me to the exclusion of everything else. Then she rallied; she wanted to go back to Thornton Hall and share her happiness. We went back. For two weeks.

She would want me to add that Mrs Tirrell is back

home. Mrs Gorman died peacefully in her sleep, a grin on her face, her teeth elsewhere. Staff Nurse Linda Casey married Doctor Douglas Beamish on what would have been Fanny's seventeenth birthday. I attended. Penny Davis was succesful in gaining two Advanced Level certificates of education and is going to Bristol University next year. Stella will miss her. Incredibly, she is learning to type.

I am working in the family business. I go to Thornton Hall every Sunday. There are things I can do there. Rosie is still alive and has some of Fanny's happiness. Dennis is improving. One day he might walk. When it rains we go outside and tip back our heads and drink the rain. Roger Parrish visits too very occasionally. He has married his secretary and finds it difficult to talk to me.

For five months of my life I knew Frances Adamson.

Hardly any time at all, yet a life time. Almost nothing. Yet everything. Sweet Fanny Adams. Sweet F.A.

ONE MORE RIVER
Lynne Reid Banks

Life in Canada had always been safe and happy for Lesley Shelby, but then her father announced that they were going to Israel, and everything changed. This is the story of their hard new life in the Kibbutz on the banks of the River Jordan, and of the stresses and strains of her secret friendship with an Arab boy whose loyalty to his people is at war with his love for her.

WHY DIDN'T THEY TELL THE HORSES?
Christine McKenna

Actress Christine McKenna had never been on a horse in her life, apart from an endearing donkey on the sands at the age of three. So when she landed the star role of the hunting and riding Christina in the TV serial, *Flambards*, some incredible experiences were ahead of her. This is the good-natured, frequently hilarious story of one diminutive actress and her relationship with a host of horses . . . some cooperative, some disdainful, and many stars in their own right.

THE FORTUNATE FEW

Tim Kennemore

Sold at an early age to professional clubs, starved to the perfect weight and worked to the point of collapse – this is the face of athletic girls with talent in the not-too-distant future. Jodie Bell is a product of this regime – determined, successful and rich. At fourteen, she is sold to Shepherds Bushwhackers. With just two years left at the top, this is her big chance. But two years is surely enough time in which to make a lot of money, and that's all she's interested in, isn't it?

THE GIRL WHO WANTED A BOY

Paul Zindel

At 15, Sibella has stringy blonde hair, a gift for fixing electrical and mechanical things, and an ambition to open her own petrol garage. But the one thing she really wants is a boy . . .

FLAMBARDS DIVIDED

K. M. Peyton

The old ivy-covered house of Flambards has seen much upheaval and tragedy since Christina first rode up the long drive as a young girl of twelve. Most important of all, her beloved Will is dead – killed in action in France – and the war is almost over. It's time, or so it seems, for Christina to marry Dick and for the two of them to settle in at the farm. But before long Will's brother, Mark, is back from the war and has cause more than anyone else to resent Dick's new position as master of the house. And it is not only Flambards that is divided but Christina herself – in her feelings for two very different men.

THE ENDLESS STEPPE

Esther Hautzig

Esther was 10 years old when, in 1941, she and her family were arrested by the Russians and transported to Siberia. This is the true story of the next five years spent in exile, of how the family kept their courage high, though they went barefoot and hungry. A magnificent book which will live long in the memory of any reader.